"Did I miss something?" she said.

Jake let out his breath in a ragged sigh.

"I'm sorry. It's just—watching you like that—you don't make it easy. You're a beautiful woman, Lydia. I can't just switch off my feelings simply because it's all over between us."

"Is it?" she said softly.

He stopped dead. "Is what?" he asked, hardly able to believe his ears.

"Is it all over? The way you kissed me last night—I rather thought it might not be."

**Almost at the altar—
will these *nearlyweds* become *newlyweds*?**

Welcome to Nearlyweds, our miniseries featuring
the ultimate romantic occasion—weddings!
Yet these are no ordinary weddings: our beautiful brides
and gorgeous grooms only *nearly* make it to the altar—
before fate intervenes and the wedding's...*off!*

But the story doesn't end there....
Find out what happens in these tantalizingly
emotional novels by some of your best-loved
Harlequin Romance® authors.

This month, enjoy a lively chase to the altar
in popular author Caroline Anderson's
The Impetuous Bride

THE IMPETUOUS BRIDE

Caroline Anderson

HARLEQUIN®

TORONTO • NEW YORK • LONDON
AMSTERDAM • PARIS • SYDNEY • HAMBURG
STOCKHOLM • ATHENS • TOKYO • MILAN • MADRID
PRAGUE • WARSAW • BUDAPEST • AUCKLAND

With thanks to Mike and Jessamy, Tamsin and Will for an inspirational setting and for "lending" me your wedding.

ISBN 0-373-03676-0

THE IMPETUOUS BRIDE

First North American Publication 2001.

PROLOGUE

'I CAN'T do this.'

'What? Lydia, don't be so silly. All you have to do is stand there, looking beautiful, and kiss everyone and say it's lovely to see them. Of course you can do it,' her mother said flatly. 'Now, Melanie, you'll be standing here, and Tom, you'll be here—'

'Mum!'

Her mother sighed and turned back. 'What is it, darling? What on earth is the problem?'

Lydia took a deep, steadying breath, and said loudly, 'I can't do this. Not the reception line thing, the marriage thing. I can't do it.'

There was a second of shocked silence, and everyone turned to look at her—her mother, clutching her clipboard like a ruffled hen hanging on to a perch; her father, jerked out of his boredom into confusion; her sister, Melanie, aghast and fascinated; Tom, the best man, his jaw dropping slightly in astonishment—and Jake. Her dear, darling Jake, who was marrying her on a whim.

She met his eyes—his beautiful, stunningly blue eyes, so full of fun and teasing laughter usually, now shuttered and expressionless, his mouth a grim line in his stony face.

'Jake, I'm sorry,' she said softly. 'Can we talk about this?'

'I think that would be a good idea,' her mother

rushed in, and hustled them out of the marquee. 'You go and talk it over, and come back when you're ready.'

Lydia didn't think she'd ever be ready. The heat was closing in on her, and yet she felt chilled to the bone. Hot and cold, like a baked Alaska. Oh, God.

Jake's hand was firm on the small of her back, and he wheeled her out into the sunshine and turned to face her.

'OK, let's have it,' he said tightly.

He was angry. She should have expected it, but she wasn't. She hadn't had time to work out her own feelings, never mind anyone else's. She'd just felt this huge pressure on her, and her mouth had just opened and spoken.

'I'm sorry,' she said again. 'I just feel—I don't know, railroaded. I think we've rushed into this and don't know how we feel, and it's all sort of happening to us. I feel acted on, and I shouldn't. I should feel as if it's our wedding, but I feel like we're actors, and I don't know if we're really doing it or just playing a part—going through the motions, you know? I just don't feel sure any more.'

He scanned her face, his eyes still expressionless, and then looked down, his toe idly scuffing the edge of the matting laid down for the endless guests that were expected in just forty-eight hours.

Guests for a wedding that might not now take place.

Oh, Lord, talk to me, she thought. Tell me I'm wrong. Tell me it's rubbish. Tell me you love me, that you want to marry me. Tell me not to worry. 'Jake?' she whispered, agonised.

He looked back at her, and for a moment she thought she saw a flicker of emotion, but then it was gone. 'If that's what you feel, then you're probably right,' he said, and his voice sounded strangely distant. 'Goodbye, Lydia. Take care of yourself.'

And he turned on his heel and strode away, up the sloping lawn towards the house. Away from her.

She stared at him, shocked. She wanted to run after him, beg and plead and reason, but it was pointless. He didn't want her. If he'd wanted her, he would have said so.

'Darling?'

She turned and fell into her father's arms, huge racking sobs tearing her chest apart, and then after a moment she turned and ran away, up to the house. She wasn't following Jake. There was no point. She just had to get away, to distance herself from the sympathy and curiosity and absolute pandemonium that would ensue.

Her bag was almost packed ready for her honeymoon in Bermuda. She tipped it out, threw back the swimming things and one or two nice outfits, grabbed her shorts and T-shirts from the drawer and hastily packed a few lightweight things. Her passport was ready—in her maiden name, still, because they hadn't thought about it until it was too late.

Good job, too, she thought, and scrubbed her eyes again so she could see. Shoes—walking shoes, comfy shoes, sandals. She didn't know where she was going, but somewhere. Somewhere far away.

'Lydia? Darling, what on earth is the matter?'

'Not now, Mum. I'll ring you.'

'Ring me? Darling, what are you doing? Where are you going?'

Her voice was rising, verging on hysteria, and Lydia just had to get out.

'I don't know. I'll ring you and let you know. I'll get a standby flight—'

'Flight?'

The word was laced with panic, and it was too much for Lydia. She scooped up her car keys, her case and her bag, checked for her passport again and kissed her mother's cheek. 'I'll be fine. I'm sorry. I just—

'Couldn't do it.' Melanie spoke from the doorway, her face sad. 'I'm sorry, love. Want to talk?'

She shook her head, blinking back the tears. 'No. Just let me go. I'm fine.'

She pushed past them, ran downstairs and bumped into Tom in the hall. 'Where's Jake?' he asked softly, and she shrugged.

'Pass. Gone home, I suppose.' She pulled off her engagement ring and held it out, her hand shaking like a leaf. 'Could you give him this, please? And, Tom—tell him I'm sorry.'

She ran past him, her eyes flooding again, smack into her father's broad and comforting chest. 'Don't do anything rash. Have you got enough money?' he asked her, and she nodded.

'I'll get by. I'm going to Heathrow Airport to start with. I don't know where after that.'

He took the keys gently out of her hand and put them on the hook on the wall. 'I'll drive you,' he said, in that quiet voice that brooked no argument.

It took two hours. He turned off the mobile phone,

turned on the radio and didn't once try to talk her out of it. It was just as well; he would have been wasting his breath.

He dropped her at one of the terminals, tucked a handful of notes into her handbag and kissed her goodbye, his brown eyes gentle with understanding. 'Keep in touch, darling. Love you.'

She swallowed hard and kissed him back. 'Love you, too. I'm sorry.'

She walked into the terminal without looking back, checked out the standby situation at the first desk that caught her eye, and within an hour she was on a flight for Thailand.

She'd never felt more alone in her life.

CHAPTER ONE

'THANKS.'

Lydia shut the door of the taxi, hitched her backpack up on to one shoulder and turned towards the house, a mixture of dread and eager anticipation tangling in her chest.

It hadn't changed at all. The roses tumbled in cheerful profusion over the Georgian façade, and the windowframes gleamed brilliant white against the soft old-rose of the bricks. A light wind from the river drifted across the sweeping lawns and caressed her skin with the scent of wild honeysuckle, and she looked down towards the soft blue-green haze of the willows on the riverbank and sighed.

Home, sweet home.

It was June—just a year since she'd left without a backward glance, and now she was back for Melanie's wedding. The irony brought a twisted little smile to her lips as she headed down towards the house, her backpack bumping against her thighs.

Only one thing was different. There was no Labrador bouncing round her, butting her hand for attention and smiling up at her, tongue lolling, because two months ago their beloved Molly had fallen asleep one night and failed to wake. It seemed strange without her—strange and empty.

The kitchen door was hanging open—just as well, really, as she didn't have her keys, but the house was usually open and if not there was always a key on the shelf in the old milking parlour.

She went in through the open door, dropped her backpack by the fridge and pulled open the door. She needed a drink. Everything else could wait.

He'd known it was going to happen, of course. Known she'd come back for Melanie's wedding, if nothing else. He'd been prepared for that, been prepared for seeing her again and steeled himself against it.

Or at least he thought he had. Now, though, his body ground to a halt for an endless moment, then went into overdrive. His heart pounded, his mouth dried, his gut clenched, and need, deep and hot and urgent, ripped through him.

She was wearing shorts—little skimpy cut-off jeans above skinny brown legs and bare feet in leather sandals. Well, maybe not skinny, but impossibly slender. Thinner than they had been, anyway. Fragile. Her T-shirt was loose and baggy, but even so he could tell she'd lost weight. Had she been ill?

Concern for her overtook the raging need, and the complex mix of emotions threatened to choke him.

She'd taken a carton of orange juice from the fridge and was draining the glass when she noticed him. Her hand trembled, and she set it down abruptly. 'Jake,' she said simply, and a tentative and rather forlorn smile tugged at her lips. 'How are you?'

Not ready for this. Not ready for that voice, soft and low and sexy, that had haunted his dreams.

'I'm fine,' he lied. 'How are you? Good journey? We were wondering when you'd arrive.'

She shrugged, picking up the empty glass, toying with it. 'OK journey, I suppose. Long flight, delays, and so on. It's nice to be home.'

'Your parents are in the drawing room with Melanie and Tom. They'll have my guts if I keep you talking out here. You'd better go and see them.'

She nodded, put down the glass and headed towards him. He was standing in the doorway, and she hesitated for a moment because he didn't move.

He didn't know why he didn't move, just that he didn't—couldn't, really, until he'd done this one, foolish thing.

He reached out and cupped her chin, bent his head and brushed a feather-soft kiss across her moist, dewy lips.

'Welcome home, Lydia,' he said softly, and then dropping her as if she might burn him he pushed past her and went out of the back door and into the sunlight. He dragged in a lungful of the fresh clean air, and closed his eyes. He could taste the sweet citrus tang of the orange juice on her lips, and the white heat of his response shocked him.

He'd really, really thought he was over her, but he wasn't. He still wanted her every bit as much as he ever had—maybe more. There was nothing like a bit of abstinence to make the heart grow fonder, he mocked himself. Still, she was back, and he was going to have to deal with it.

Well, fine. He could. Just so long as he remembered she'd walked away before, and she'd do it again. She was trouble—big trouble, with a capital T, and he wasn't going to fall for her charms again.

Ever.

*   *   *

Lydia stood rooted to the spot for an age, her fingers pressed to her lips, her eyes wide with surprise. She should have expected him to be here, should have expected that he would still have this effect on her.

She'd known he'd be at the wedding, of course, but it had never occurred to her that he'd be here in her parents' house—just sitting around chatting, for heaven's sake!

Even if he did live just next door.

Oh, damn.

Of course he'd be here. He was Tom's oldest friend. They'd known each other from birth, practically. Of course he was about.

'Jake, can't you find it—? Darling!'

She found herself engulfed in her mother's hug, and the next second the others were there, laughing and crying and hugging, and then there was Tom, looking over Melanie's shoulder towards the door.

'Has Jake gone?' he asked, sounding surprised.

She nodded. 'Yes. He bumped into me on the way out.' She looked towards the door, puzzled. Well, she'd assumed he'd been on the way out—or had he left because of her?

There was a moment of awkward silence, then her father hugged her again. 'Oh, it's lovely to have you back, poppet. Are you all right?'

'I'm fine,' she lied, her eyes still lingering on the door. She dragged her attention back to her family, and linked arms with her father and sister. 'Absolutely fine. It's lovely to be home. Now, come on, I want to hear about the wedding plans. Tell me all.'

Melanie laughed self-consciously. 'It'll all be horribly familiar,' she said with a wry grimace, and Lydia's heart sank.

Of course. Mel had thrown herself into planning Lydia's wedding last year, and throughout Lydia had been acutely aware that it was not really the wedding she'd wanted. The marquee by the river, the elaborate flowers, the little gilt chairs, the round tables with their snowy cloths and sparkling tableware—it had always been Mel's wedding.

Lydia had wanted to get married under the willow with just a very few immediate family, and have a picnic by the river with champagne and soft, ripe cheeses and sweet, juicy grapes.

Instead Melanie had gone into a huddle with her mother and come up with a three-course meal and elaborate seating plans and a guest list that left no one out.

Jake had smiled tolerantly, and Lydia had felt powerless to resist.

Until the very end.

And now, like some kind of awful joke, it was all going to be re-enacted, but this time the cast would change places and the curtain wouldn't come down until after the final act.

And she and Jake would have to endure the parody of their wedding, and pretend enthusiasm and delight for the benefit of their loved ones.

Suddenly she found herself wishing she'd stayed away for another month and come home when it was all over.

'So, tell us all about your travels,' her mother said, settling back with an expectant smile. 'We've had such brief contact, you naughty girl.'

Lydia grinned sheepishly. 'Sorry. I just needed to get right away.'

'We understand. So—tell all. Where have you come from now? We could hardly keep up with you.'

'Australia—well, via Singapore. I stopped off to see a few friends.'

'So tell us all about it,' her father instructed. 'You went to Thailand first when I dropped you off at the airport, is that right?'

She nodded. 'Yes, and I just bummed around for a month and tried to sort myself out, then I had to leave because I didn't have a visa, so I went to India and worked in a hotel as a courier, then I went to Singapore, and Bali, then over to Australia, on to New Zealand and back to Australia, just doing anything I could find for cash and a roof over my head.'

Her mother closed her eyes. 'It sounds so dangerous.'

It had been, of course, but there was no way she was telling her mother about the foreign tourist who'd tried to rape her in India, or the girl in New Zealand who'd stolen everything except her photos, her passport and the clothes she'd had on.

'It was fun,' she said, ignoring the hard work and the hunger pangs and the dysentery. What they didn't know wouldn't hurt them, she decided, and anyway, she'd survived and learned a few vital lessons.

'You're skinny,' her father said bluntly, scanning her legs.

She curled them tighter under her and laughed lightly. 'Nonsense. It's just because I'm brown. So, tell, me, how's business?' she asked her mother, deftly switching the subject.

'Brilliant. We've done several new projects—Dunham Hall, the Priory at Whitfield—loads. You would have loved Dunham. We did a stunning authentic kitchen and a fabulous butler's pantry. It's like a time warp. I've got all the photos; I'll show you later. I just need to ring the florist before I forget, and give her some answers. Raymond, could you go through it with me again, please, darling? It's only a week; we really must sort it out.'

Which brought Lydia back to the reason for her return. As her parents went out, she looked at Melanie and Tom, sprawled comfortably on the sofa together, Tom's arm draped possessively around Mel's shoulders, and she gave an inward sigh. She couldn't envy them their happiness. It had been within reach, and she'd walked away.

'So, lovebirds, when did you decide to tie the knot?' she asked, striving for a light tone.

'About a year ago,' Tom confessed with a smile. 'When I first met her in the run-up to your wedding. I took one look at her, and I thought, That's my woman.'

'Caveman stuff, eh?' Lydia teased, wishing she'd been anything like as sure of Jake as Mel clearly was of Tom—because, of course, if she had been, she would have stayed and married him.

'Oh, I like caveman tactics,' Mel said with a chuckle, laughing up at him. 'I love it when he gets all masterful. Makes him think he's boss, and he enjoys that.'

Lydia laughed at Tom's resigned smile. She guessed her quicksilver high-spirited sister ran rings round the straightforward and honest man she'd chosen, but he was generous enough to indulge her.

If only she'd had so open a relationship with Jake, but for some reason they'd never really broken through the surface and shared anything on a really deep level. Perhaps that was the problem.

Perhaps, she thought, that was the only problem. Maybe if they'd really talked to each other, got to know each other better, she would have known if he'd loved her.

Tom was getting to his feet. 'I have to go—things to sort out with Jake. I'll be back later. Lydia, come out with us for dinner. We're going to a new trattoria in town.'

'We?'

'Us and Jake.'

She wrinkled her nose. 'I don't know. He might not want me there.'

Tom blinked. 'Don't be silly. That's all water under the bridge now. He won't mind.'

Lydia wasn't so sure, but then she'd never been sure of Jake. 'I'll see,' she compromised.

He bent and gave Mel a lingering and tender kiss, and then went out, leaving the two sisters alone for the first time.

Mel, direct as ever, looked across at her and said bluntly, 'You look like hell. You're too thin, your eyes are tired and you look sad. Has it really been that bloody a year?'

And, for no very good reason that she could think of, Lydia burst into tears. In an instant Mel was perched on the arm of the chair and her arms were round Lydia, and she was being hugged and comforted by someone who really loved her. Lord, how she'd missed that! She slid her arms round Mel's waist and hugged her back.

'It's good to be home,' she said a little damply, and Mel shoved a tissue in her hand and smoothed her hair back off her brow.

'Are you going to be OK about Jake?' she asked gently, and Lydia shrugged.

'I don't know. I thought so, but seeing him just now—I don't know any more. Has he said anything about me coming back?'

She shook her head. 'Not really—not to me, and not to Tom, if what he just said is anything to go by. I don't suppose you have to see that much of him, really, if you don't want to.'

'Mmm.' If she didn't. The trouble was, she wasn't at all sure that not seeing him was what she *did* want. She'd missed him endlessly this last year, and seeing him now had brought it all back. She blinked back another wave of tears and straightened up.

'Has he—um—you know—?'

'Got another woman?' Mel smiled understandingly. 'No. Not that I've heard about, and Tom would have told me if he'd known. He's been in London a lot, of course. He's hardly here at all—well, nor's Tom, of course, but I spend a lot of time in London with him when Mum can spare me, which isn't that often. The business has really taken off in the last year—she's delighted you're back, by the way.' Mel shot her a keen look. 'I take it you are back?'

Lydia shrugged. 'I don't know. Probably, but I don't know if I'll stay here. Not with Jake next door.'

'Well, that's not a problem; the house is up for sale. He's moving away.'

'What?' Lydia felt as if the bottom had fallen out of her world. 'He's what?' she repeated, shocked, and then realised just how much her feelings about coming home had been to do with Jake. He couldn't be moving away. She'd never see him again—

'He's going to stay in London—like I said, he's hardly ever here now.'

Never here? Oh, Lord. She stood up, patting Mel on the shoulder in passing. 'I'm going out for a walk,' she said, and went blindly into the kitchen, past the place where he'd kissed her just now in the doorway of the room where he'd proposed to her just over a year ago, the room where so many of her hopes and dreams had been formed, only to come crashing down around her ears.

She ran down through the garden, over the lawn, under the rose arch and down to the wildflower meadow by the river where the marquee would be put up in just a few days.

Her willow was there, the tips of the branches trailing in the water, and she leant against the trunk and dragged in a shaky breath, and then another.

He couldn't go.

The river swam out of focus, and she slid down the trunk and plopped on to the damp grass, dropping her head back against the rough bark and closing her eyes. The tears slipped unheeded down her cheeks, and she wished she could turn back time and change the course of the last year.

Maybe if she'd married him, given him a chance, all her doubts and fears could have been ironed out.

Maybe they would have learned to talk to each other, learned to open up their hearts and dared to share their feelings.

And maybe then, instead of a dull and endless ache inside, she would have been filled with joy and contentment, like Mel.

She turned her head and looked towards Jake's house, and then she saw him, standing by the river on his side of the fence, watching her. He was too far away to see her tears, but he lifted his hand and waved, and turned away.

She wanted to run after him, to ask him if he'd loved her, really loved her, or if he'd just allowed himself to be manoeuvred into the whole wedding thing.

She didn't, though. She didn't move. Instead she sat there and watched him until the tears blinded her again and he was gone.

What was she doing there? He stood for an age, watching her leaning against the tree, her face tipped up to the dappled sun, and he ached to hold her.

You're a fool, he told himself. She's no good for you. She's just a beautiful butterfly, and if you trap her she'll die as surely as if you put a pin through her heart.

He glanced at his watch. There was someone coming to see the house at four—just an hour away. He had to go and tidy the kitchen—the kitchen Lydia had designed and installed, the kitchen she'd planned as if it were her own.

She was everywhere in it. Every finishing touch, every clever little idea screamed her name. That was one reason why he was selling up. That and her return. Watching her day after day flitting about the place, hearing that beautiful tinkling laugh, watching her run to her car with those never-ending, gorgeous legs flashing in the sun—

He'd had dreams about those legs tangling with his, entwined around his waist as he buried himself deep inside her.

He growled impatiently, and she looked up, straight at him. She was too far away to read her expression, but he couldn't stay there in case she came over and read the yearning in his eyes.

He lifted his hand in a casual salute and turned away, walking back to the house with a heavy heart. He couldn't let her do this to him. He couldn't wallow in self-pity like this or he just wouldn't survive.

He had this week to get through, and the wedding next Saturday, a week today, and then he wouldn't have to see her again. He could leave the house. Packers could clear it and bring the things he wanted to London, and the rest could be sold.

And maybe then he could move on.

'Lydia? Tonight?' Jake gave what he hoped was a casual shrug, and tried to ignore the sudden lurching of his heart. 'Sure. Why should I mind?'

'Well, that's what I said,' Tom replied. 'Anyway, whatever, you're going to have to see each other this week so you might as well get used to it.'

'Absolutely. It's not a problem,' he assured Tom, hoping it was true. 'How are the plans going?'

'Oh, pretty smooth. There's a lot to do, but, having

just had a dry run, as it were, I don't suppose it's as bad as it could have been.'

Jake winced inwardly. A dry run? Was that how they viewed the disastrous mess last year had been?

'It could have been a simpler affair,' he pointed out, and Tom gave a rueful laugh.

'With Mel orchestrating it? Not a chance. My darling girl wants all the bells and whistles, and that's what she's having. It seems to be a family failing.'

Except, of course, that Lydia had looked increasingly unhappy with it—or with him? He didn't know. He hadn't stopped to find out.

'What time are we going out?' he asked now, and Tom shrugged.

'Seven-thirty? Table's booked for eight-thirty, but we could go for a drink first.'

'Fine. I'll be ready. Right, stick that mug in the dishwasher and get out of here. I've got viewers coming to see the house in ten minutes and I need to check it. How's your room?'

'It's fine. Lord, man, you're such a nag.'

'Check it.'

Tom saluted, vaulted off the edge of the worktop, dropped his mug in the dishwasher with a clatter and sauntered out into the hall. Jake shook his head, wiped down the worktop again, took a last look round and headed for the hall.

Fresh flowers stood in a huge vase on the side table, the sun was streaming into the drawing room windows and it looked good. He heard Tom coming downstairs two at a time, humming.

'Well?'

'Spotless. It'll knock 'em dead.' Tom punched him

affectionately on the shoulder and headed out through the back door, just as the front doorbell rang.

They loved it. Everyone who'd looked at it loved it. There was going to be a mammoth fight over it, apparently, and the agent predicted that it would go to sealed bids, with people making their best and final offers at some time in the next week or two.

Well, at least it wouldn't hang on, he thought heavily, closing the door behind the viewers at shortly after five. They'd wanted to look at everything several times, and he'd sent them off on their own and then had to listen to them raving about the kitchen for a good ten minutes.

Every little feature that Lydia had factored in, the woman had picked up on. The convenient way the trays slotted into units and became part of the fabric, the ingenious way the cupboards hinged out to give access to the back, the huge and practical work island with a granite area for pastry-making inset into the solid mahogany top, the butcher's block set into another area—she'd loved them all.

She'd loved the deep butler's sink under the window, the decorative tiling behind the Aga, the butler's pantry with its stone shelves and floor-to-ceiling storage—all of it, each scrap of worktop and every single knob had been commented on and caressed lovingly.

She'd been particularly interested in the space under the worktop in the side of the island nearest the Aga.

'It's a dog bed,' Jake had explained.

She'd blinked and looked at it, then at him. 'It is?'

'Potentially. I've had to spend more and more time

in London, though, and the dog wouldn't have fitted in,' he'd explained economically.

'Oh, how sad. Our dog would love it, so near the Aga. What a clever idea. Still, maybe one day you'll be able to have your dog.'

Jake had done the only thing he could—he had smiled and nodded and tried not to grind his teeth too loudly.

And now, finally, they were gone, after one last look round the upstairs, and he was on his own. He went into the drawing room, dropped into his favourite chair and sighed.

Why the hell had she had to come back?

Lydia wasn't at all sure about going out that evening. She'd fallen into bed at three-thirty, and to her surprise she'd slept soundly till seven. Now Mel was sitting on her bed shoving a cup of tea in her hand and telling her to get up and come out, it would do her good and they had so little time left before she was married.

That wasn't how it felt to Lydia. The week ahead stretched away into the hereafter, as far as she was concerned, and she couldn't see any way round it. That being the case, she might as well get used to it. She threw the bedclothes off, slid out of bed and put the tea down to cool.

'I'll come,' she agreed. 'How dressy is it?'

'Anything—I'm wearing a casual silk trouser suit.'

Lydia rolled her eyes. 'I have shorts—that's about it.'

'You have loads of clothes!'

'And none of them will fit. I'm thinner, Mel.'

'Not that much thinner. Let's see—here, look, this is nice and it fits where it touches. Wear that.'

Jake's favourite dress. Oh, hell. She sighed, dropped the dress on to the bed and headed for the bathroom. 'OK. Give me five.'

It took longer, of course, because her hair needed washing, but luckily the tan covered the shadows round her eyes, so she slapped on a bit of smoky eyeshadow, a flick of mascara and a dash of soft pink lipstick, and then shimmied into the dress.

It still looked good. It was long and soft and floaty, and she just hoped that Jake wouldn't remember it was what she'd been wearing when he'd proposed to her.

It was that dress. Damn. Of all the things she could have worn, it had to be that one. He'd had fantasies about her in it, standing with the wind blowing it against her body and lovingly outlining every curve.

Not that she'd have many curves to outline now, he thought, studying her critically. Without the baggy T-shirt he could see the slender arms and narrow waist, the small, high breasts and, when she moved, the angle of her hipbone.

She wasn't wearing a bra. She usually didn't—with the breasts that she scornfully described as two grapes on a chopping board she hardly needed to, but the cool night air had pebbled her nipples and he wished she'd put a jumper on before he disgraced himself.

'Right, are we ready?' Tom asked, hugging Mel to his side, and Lydia nodded.

'I'm starving. I hate aeroplane food.' She yawned

hugely, and then laughed. 'Sorry. I was in bed. Mel dug me out half an hour ago.'

In bed. Wonderful. Just what he needed. Between that and her pert little nipples, he was going to make an idiot of himself for sure. He tugged his heavy cotton sweater down and just prayed that it wouldn't get too hot in the restaurant.

The atmosphere was dreadful. Mel and Tom did their best to keep the mood light, but Lydia was too tired to join in really and Jake, working his way steadily through the wine, was grimly silent.

Until the coffee was served, that was, and then he sprawled back in his chair, one arm coiled round the back, and regarded her levelly as he stirred his sugarless black coffee with unwarranted determination.

'So, Lydia, do tell—did you "find yourself" on the hippy trail?'

'Hippy trail?' she said, trying not to wince at the coldness of his tone. 'I met a lot of very interesting people—very nice people. I made some wonderful friends, and learned a great deal about trust and team work and sharing. And you? What have you done in the last year?'

'Oh, turned over a few more companies, stripped a few assets, trashed a few lives—you know the sort of thing.'

'Nothing worthwhile, then,' she quipped, hating herself even while she knew it was just self-defence.

He laughed coldly. 'Absolutely not—not compared to dumping my fiancé just before the wedding and disappearing off round the world like an irresponsible child. I'm amazed you haven't come back reeking of patchouli and covered in multiple body piercings.'

She closed her eyes briefly, reeling from the shock of his unwarranted attack. Well, maybe not unwarranted, but totally out of character—wasn't it? Tom seemed to think so. He jerked upright and glowered at his old friend. 'Hell, Jake, that's a bit harsh,' he said.

'Is it? The woman jilts me two days before our wedding and you say *I'm* harsh? I don't think so.'

Lydia felt hot colour scorch her cheeks. Her heart was pounding and she thought she was going to be sick. She just had to get out of there, away from him and his bitterness and hatred before it destroyed the crumbling veneer around her and exposed her pain. She looked round desperately at Mel.

'If you don't mind, I think I'll get a taxi home. I don't really want this coffee, and I'm tired.' She stood up, conscious that Jake, who last year would have stood up without fail, was still sprawled in the chair scowling into his cup. 'I'll see you tomorrow.'

'Tom, take her home,' Mel said hurriedly.

'No, we'll all go,' Jake said, standing up abruptly and pulling his wallet out. 'There's no point pretending we're having fun.' He dropped a handful of notes on the table, nodded to the waiter and headed for the door, his coffee untouched.

'Is everything all right?' the waiter asked anxiously, fluttering round them, and Tom soothed him.

'It's fine. We're just rather tired. Thank you.'

He put a proprietorial arm around Lydia's shoulders, and led her out of the door. Mel was ahead of them, steaming after Jake and giving him hell, if

Lydia's guess was right. Oh, damn. She should have stayed at home in bed and not come out with them. It was foolish to expect that they could be civil.

It might be water under the bridge by now, as Tom had said, but it had been a tidal wave, and the bridge was damaged beyond repair.

He seemed so angry still. That puzzled her, because for all she'd felt she didn't really know him, she'd known that much about him, and he wasn't a vindictive or unkind person.

So why, then, was he so angry? Unless it was because he still cared about her. And if he still cared that much, if he was still so angry, then maybe he really *had* loved her. It might just have been wounded pride, of course, but if not, was it really too late, or was there still a chance for them to mend the bridge?

Lydia didn't know. All she knew was that she had a week in which to find out—a week that only hours ago had seemed to stretch on for ever, and now seemed nothing like long enough...

CHAPTER TWO

JAKE was standing by the front passenger door of Tom's car, but Mel elbowed him out of the way.

'You can sit in the back with my sister and apologise for bitching at each other, or get a taxi. Right now I don't much care which, but I'd be grateful if you'd manage to behave towards each other in a civilised fashion. I'm not asking you to be buddies, clearly that's too much, but you could at least be polite.'

And she slid into the front seat, slammed the door and left them standing by the car in silence.

After an endless moment, Jake reached for the handle, opened the door and held it for her without a word. Still in silence, Lydia climbed into the back and slid across the seat, and he folded himself in beside her, fastened his seat belt and stared straight ahead.

'Sorry, Lydia. Sorry, Jake.'

They both glared at Mel. 'Butt out, little sister,' Lydia said tightly. 'I can fight my own battles.'

'Nevertheless, I think—'

'Drop it, Mel,' Tom said, and started the car, turning the radio on. Lydia realised she was shaking all over, hanging on by a thread, and she could feel the waves of tension coming off Jake.

They'd driven about two tense and emotionally charged miles before he sighed and turned to her. 'I'm sorry,' he said tightly. 'I didn't mean to snipe at you. I just find this very difficult.'

He wasn't alone! She'd been wondering for ages just why she'd let herself be talked into this calculated disaster of an evening. 'It's OK,' she conceded, desperate to end this war that had sprung up between them. 'I never expected you to kill the fatted calf.' She tried a tentative smile, and his mouth flickered just briefly.

It wasn't a smile, but it was a concession, and the tension eased noticeably, to her huge relief. She relaxed back against the seat, still shaking with reaction, but at least they were nearly home.

They pulled up on the drive a few minutes later, and Tom cut the engine. 'Coffee?' Mel suggested, and gave them both a considering look over the back of the seat. 'Think you two can cope with that?'

'I should think we'll manage,' Jake said drily, and, opening the door, he got out and helped Mel from the car, leaving Tom to open Lydia's door.

He gave her shoulder a quick squeeze and smiled at her worriedly. 'You OK?' he asked softly, and she nodded.

'Yes, I'm fine. Come on in, it's chilly.'

She rubbed her bare arms briskly to warm them, and led the way into the kitchen. The Aga was warm, as ever, and she put the kettle on automatically and leant against the front rail, her back to the stove and her hands wrapped round the rail for warmth.

Her mother came into the kitchen and commandeered Mel and Tom immediately, leaving her alone with Jake, and she was suddenly conscious of the way she was standing and the way Jake was looking at her. Dear God, did he think she was being deliberately provocative?

She crossed her arms over her chest, her fingers gripping her upper arms defensively, and gave him a cautious smile. 'I'm sorry about Mel,' she began, but he cut her off with a short, humourless laugh.

'No. She was right. I apologise. It was unforgivable. I shouldn't have poked fun at you; you have every right to do what you like with your life.'

'Not if it hurts other people,' she murmured softly.

He was silent, his eyes expressionless, and then he turned away, reaching for the mugs with a familiarity that tore at her heart. How many times had she watched him do that? Struggling to fill the silence, she groped for a topic. 'How did you get on with the house this afternoon?' she asked. 'Were the people OK?'

He gave her a strange look. 'We discussed this over dinner,' he reminded her, and she coloured.

'I meant, did you like them? Would you like them to have your house? It's a very personal thing selling something you've worked hard on and care about— you want to make sure it goes into the right hands.'

'It's a house, Lydia,' he said in a tight voice. 'Just a house.'

She shrugged and pulled the kettle off the hob, lowering the cover down over the hotplate with exaggerated care. 'Coffee or tea?'

'Coffee—thank you.' He set the mugs down beside her, and his arm brushed hers, bringing lingering warmth to the cold skin. He was so close she could smell the faint citrus scent of his aftershave, so familiar it made her ache to hold him, to slip into his arms and rest her weary head on his chest and cry her eyes out for all the stupid things she'd done in the last year.

Instead she moved away, out of range of the scent of his body, and made the coffee with brisk and economical movements. 'I'll take theirs into the study— I can tell this is going to be one of those long confabs that will drag on for ages.'

She put four mugs on a tray and carried them through, earning distracted smiles of thanks, and went back to the kitchen.

Jake was sitting at the table, his long fingers curled around his mug, staring down into its murky contents as if it held the secret of eternal life. There was a box of mint crisp chocolates on the side and she offered him one. He shook his head, but she had two, dipping them in her coffee and sucking them. It was a disgusting habit, but they tasted better like that and she was hardly trying to impress him.

Just as well, judging by the strange way he was looking at her.

'They liked it,' he said abruptly, and she paused in her sucking and looked at him in utter confusion.

'They? They liked what?'

'The viewers,' he explained. 'They liked your kitchen. She waxed lyrical on every single feature. I thought she was going to rip out the dog bed and take it with her.'

Lydia smiled wryly. 'Oh, dear. Still, I suppose it's a good sign.'

'Oh, absolutely. The agent seems to think they'll all come to blows over it. It certainly won't hang about on the market, apparently.'

Lydia felt a great pang of regret. It would have been her house, hers and Jake's, and they would have brought their children up in it.

If their marriage had stood the test of time. Instead it had fallen even before the first hurdle.

'You ought to come and see the house before it goes,' he was saying. 'I've done a lot more since you left. It was in a pretty basic state when I bought it— I don't know if you can remember.'

Remember? How could she forget walking round the echoing emptiness with him, excitement gripping her at the thought of transforming the basic and antiquated scullery into a wonderful family kitchen that would be the heart of his beautiful home. Not for her, of course, not at that stage, but for him and some nameless woman who would become his wife.

'I want children,' he'd said, 'so nothing too precious.'

And she'd imagined the children, little blue-eyed, dark-haired clones of their father, with mischievous smiles and infectious laughter.

It was in that kitchen that he'd first kissed her...

She jerked herself back to the present and his invitation. 'I'd love to see it—and of course I remember it. It will be interesting to see what you've done.'

Heartbreaking, too, but she couldn't seem to walk away from him no matter how sensible it might be. And it could be her last chance to see it.

'When?' she asked, and he shrugged.

'Tomorrow? Come for breakfast. Your body clock will be all up the creek, so tired as you are I don't suppose you'll be able to lie in. Ring me. I'll cook for you.'

She met his eyes, and for a moment there was a glimmer of the old Jake, then it was gone again.

'Thanks,' she murmured. 'That would be lovely. Don't wait in, though. I might sleep—who knows?'

'I'll be in,' he assured her, and it sounded almost like a promise.

He must be crazy. He couldn't sit in the same room with her without being reminded of her defection, and yet he was inviting her over—and for breakfast, for heaven's sake! Not coffee, not a cup of tea, but breakfast, the most intimate meal of all—a meal they'd never shared.

He was mad. He had to be. Bringing her back into the house and filling every nook and cranny of it with her image was absolutely the last thing he needed, but it didn't matter. It wasn't as if those images would haunt him for years, because the house would be sold and she'd never even been to his new flat in London.

No, it was just a short-lived torture, a bit of flagellation that if he wasn't such a masochist he would have avoided like the plague, but he was too weak and too stupid to steer clear of her.

He drained his coffee and stood up. She was drooping over the table, struggling to keep her eyes open after her long flight, and he was keeping her up.

Not that he ought to care, but for some absurd reason he did.

'I'm off,' he said briskly. 'Go to bed. Call me in the morning.'

She stood up and went to the door with him, and without thinking he lowered his head and brushed her lips.

'Sleep tight, Princess,' he murmured roughly, and then could have kicked himself for the familiar endearment.

He walked home in the dark, striding along the lane in the faint moonlight, his body stalked by the image of her leaning against the Aga, her nipples clear against the soft fabric of her dress, the tip of her tongue chasing the last melted smear of chocolate on her lips, the gentle sway of her body as she moved.

He could still smell the light, teasing fragrance of her skin, taste the chocolate on her lips. His palms ached to cup those small, soft breasts, to cradle her bottom and lift her against him as he lost himself in her.

Damn. He stripped off his sweater and unfastened his shirt, pulling it out of his trousers and letting the cool night air to his skin. Damn her for her hold over him.

It was just because he'd never had her, of course, because she'd always held back from that last intimacy. If he'd made love to her he could have forgotten her, could have got her out of his system.

Maybe now was a chance—not out of revenge, but just as a way of purging his emotion.

And maybe he was a bigger fool than he'd thought.

He went in, slammed the door behind him and took the stairs three at a time. Maybe a cold shower would bring him to his senses.

She rang him at a quarter to nine, knowing he would be up. He was always up by six, so he'd told her in the past, and he answered the phone on the second ring.

'Hi,' he said, and his voice sounded gruff and sexy and early-morning, and did nothing for her composure.

'I'm awake,' she said unnecessarily. 'Is it too early? I'm dying for coffee.'

'Of course not. Come on round. I'll leave the back door open.'

She pulled her wet hair into a ponytail, contemplated putting on make-up and told herself not to be ridiculous. She was going for breakfast, nothing else.

Her jeans hung on her, but they would have to do. She slid her feet into sandals, tied a jumper round her shoulders in case it was chilly out and walked briskly round to his house.

Although it was next door, technically, it took a couple of minutes to walk there along the lane, and the fresh morning air felt wonderful on her skin. It had rained in the night, just lightly, and the air was cool and damp and scented with honeysuckle and roses.

It was gorgeous, so much more subtle than the exotic scents of the tropics, and Lydia felt the tension in her ease a little. Nevertheless, she approached the back door with a certain amount of trepidation. She'd put so much of herself into the design of this particular kitchen, and then later so much love into the planning of the other things they'd hoped to do, and now she would see what he had achieved—and what he was casually going to hand over to another person without a pang, because it was, in his words, 'just a house'.

Not to Lydia. Never to Lydia.

She tapped on the open door and went in, greeted

by the wonderful aroma of fresh coffee and sizzling bacon, and there he was, standing at the work island in a pair of ancient jeans faded almost to white over the knees and seat, a soft T-shirt tucked in, emphasising the breadth of his shoulders and the neatness of his waist.

'Hi,' he murmured, and threw her a smile that made her heart kick. 'Come on in.'

She went in, looking round her at the finished room, settled in now to its role and every bit as lovely as it had been. A wave of sadness washed over her, and instinctively she crossed to the Aga for the comfort of its warmth. 'Anything I can do?'

'No. I'm just about done. There's a plate of goodies in the bottom oven—you could get it out.'

She reached down and pulled out a dish heaped with bacon, sausages, tomatoes, mushrooms, tiny fried potatoes—

'Good grief,' she said faintly. 'Do you always do breakfast like this?'

He grinned, turning her heart over, and put the last few rashers of bacon on to the dish. 'Only on Sundays. There's scrambled egg in the microwave; it just needs another turn.' He pressed a couple of buttons and while it finished off he put coffee and milk and mugs on a tray. Toast popped up, the scrambled eggs were done and he was hustling her through into the breakfast room.

'Oh!' she exclaimed, slamming to a halt in the doorway. 'You did the conservatory!'

'Like it?' he asked from right behind her, and she felt her eyes fill. It had been another of their plans, and she felt the huge well of sadness grow a little larger.

'It's beautiful,' she whispered, and swallowed the lump in her throat. 'Really lovely.'

'Go on out there. I've set the table.'

She put the hot dish down on the mat in the middle of the cast-iron table, and looked around at the pretty structure. White-painted, it reached up towards the clear blue sky, the centre of the roof a square raised lantern, a typical Georgian feature and absolutely at home in the context of his house. Plants rioted around the broad sills, foamed out of huge pots and swarmed up the glass. It was like a tropical paradise, and she shook her head in astonishment.

'You must have green fingers,' she murmured, stroking a leaf thoughtfully.

'You sound surprised.'

She shrugged. Just another thing she hadn't known about him. 'It's lovely,' she said, and turned to look at him.

For a moment there was something in his eyes, something that could have been yearning, and then it was gone, replaced by a genial nothingness like a shield over his feelings.

Unless that was just fanciful imagination, which was quite likely, given her lack of sleep.

'I can't claim all the credit. I have a domestic genius who waters them for me. I suspect it's more her touch than mine.' He held a chair for her, and she sat down, looking out over the garden and noticing the little changes—the new rose bed, the repaired formal terrace, the little summer house—

'You've got a summer house!' she exclaimed.

'I know. It just seemed to need one. Come on, help yourself before it's cold.'

She looked at the mass of food and her stomach rumbled. Her last proper meal had been in Singapore, and since she'd hardly eaten a thing last night because of the atmosphere, she was utterly ravenous. 'I could eat all of this,' she confessed with a wry grin.

'Do. I can cook more. Pile in.'

She did, not stopping until her plate was clear for the second time and she was halfway down her mug of coffee. Then she leant back and smiled sheepishly. 'That was wonderful.'

His answering smile was gentle and a little sad.

'You're welcome.' He looked down into his coffee, his face thoughtful, and then looked up, spearing her with those incredible blue eyes. 'About last night— I'm sorry I was so rude.'

She shook her head. 'Forget it. We've dealt with it. It wasn't easy for me seeing you again, so I can't imagine you found it any easier. We all say things we don't mean when we're under pressure.'

He didn't reply, just nodded slightly in acknowledgement and returned his attention to his coffee.

The sun rose higher, filtering through the tree overhead and bathing them in gentle, dappled light. It was calm and restful, and she couldn't imagine why on earth he would want to sell it and return to London full-time—

'Why are you selling it?' she asked, the words just coming out without her permission. Oh, Lord, did that sound as desperate as she thought it did?

He shrugged, his lovely blue eyes unreadable. 'What is there here for me?'

Me! she wanted to scream, but she couldn't. He didn't want her; he'd made that perfectly obvious. 'Mel said you'd been spending more time in London.'

'Business has been quite busy recently,' he agreed, and pushed his chair back, his breakfast hardly touched. 'Come and see the rest of the house.'

And then she could go, she thought, and get out of his way. He was clearly in a hurry to get rid of her—probably regretted the invitation, but his natural good manners would have prevented him from withdrawing it.

She followed him back to the hall and through the rest of the house, and as she looked around she thought it seemed soulless. Only the kitchen seemed to have any real heart—the kitchen and the conservatory, which they'd planned together and researched in the run-up to the wedding.

They went upstairs and looked in the bedrooms, and they were all beautifully presented and co-ordinated. She wondered who had done it, and if he'd slept with her, and felt a surge of jealous rage.

'This is my room,' he said finally, pushing open a door, and a huge lump wedged in her throat, because this was what she'd said she wanted—the walls, carpet, curtains, all soft creamy white, with a huge four-poster in the middle, its massive barley-twist posts and heavily carved head and foot boards gleaming with the patina of age.

There was a richly embroidered cream bedspread smoothed over the quilt, piled high with cushions and pillows, and behind the headboard more of the same fabric hung in deep folds.

'Did you do the bathroom?' she asked in a choked voice, and he nodded.

'Take a look.'

It was lovely—antique fittings with brass taps, the bath a monster with huge ball and claw feet, and in the corner a real Victorian shower with heads all down the sides as well as a massive rose overhead. It must use gallons of water, but it looked wonderful.

'I got all the stuff from that reclamation yard you told me about.'

'Well done,' she said, flashing him a smile without really looking at him, because it all hurt too much and she was too close to the bed where she would have lain with him at night for the last year, and loved him.

She looked at her watch without seeing it. 'I must fly,' she said. 'I haven't really asked anything about the wedding or made myself useful at all yet, and they'll be wondering where I am.'

She headed for the door, all but running down the stairs, and at the kitchen door she turned and looked back at him, and wondered if she'd gone crazy or if that really was regret in his eyes.

'Thanks for the breakfast,' she said, and then she fled, just before her tears spilled over and gave her away...

He was mad. Certifiably, stark raving mad. Why on *earth* had he taken her into his bedroom? Now she'd know he'd hung on her every word and built her dream for her, in the vain hope that she'd come back and share it with him.

He snorted. Not a chance. She hadn't been able to

get out of there fast enough. Maybe she didn't even remember all their plans.

Not a hope. She'd realise what a fool he was, and even now she was probably laughing at him.

Well, damn her. He threw the remains of the breakfast in the bin, tossed the plates and cutlery into the dishwasher with scant regard for their safety and went out, slamming the door behind him. The coach house door slid open at the touch of a button, and he got into the car, gunned the engine and shot out of the garage, up the drive and off down the lane.

He tried to outrun his demons, but all he got for his pains was a speeding ticket and a lecture from the policeman that pulled him over. He drove to London, rang up a friend and thrashed him comprehensively at squash, then drowned his sorrows in the bar and went back to the flat to sleep it off.

Ridiculous. He never drank to excess, and yet Lydia only had to set foot in the country and two nights running he had too much to drink.

He woke up early on Monday morning, all his muscles screaming protest after the hammering he'd given them the day before, and drove back to Suffolk, arriving at his house as the sun came up over the trees and flooded the valley with gold.

He should have stayed in London. He had plenty to do in the office, but they could manage without him so long as he was accessible by phone, and the masochist in him wanted to be near Lydia for the few short days that were left.

He parked the car, went inside and made coffee, then banged on Tom's door at eight with a mug of coffee to find Mel there, too, snuggled up against his friend's side, a blissful smile on her face.

'Morning,' she said chirpily, and he dredged up a smile.

'Hi. What's on the menu today?' he asked, wondering if he could make himself indispensable and coincidentally be in Lydia's way.

'Goodness knows. I'm keeping out of it,' Mel said, winking mischievously at Tom. 'We've got better things to do.'

They were clearly going to be no help at all. He went downstairs, drained the coffee pot and checked his watch.

Eight-thirty. He loaded the dishwasher, cleaned up the kitchen and strolled next door. The craftsmen were already coming and going in the kitchen workshops over the road, and as he looked down the drive his heart kicked. Lydia was sitting with her mother outside the back door on a bench, their faces tipped up to the sun, and as his feet scrunched on the gravel they looked up and Mrs Benton waved.

'Jake! Come and have some coffee,' she called, and his heart sank. He'd had enough coffee already this morning to launch a fleet of submarines, and the last thing he wanted was any more.

'I've just had one—'

'Some orange juice, then, or a croissant? We've just put some in the Aga. Have you eaten?'

He looked at Lydia, busy looking non-committal, and wished for the thousandth time that he could read her mind and know what she was thinking.

'No, I haven't. That would be lovely, thank you, Maggie.'

Lydia got to her feet and went into the kitchen, and he followed her. 'Am I in the way?' he asked quietly, and she stiffened and then laughed softly.

'Of course not. Go on out and find a table and chairs from round the corner and drag them into the sun, could you? We'll eat outside, it's so nice.'

He went, as commanded, and then sat with Maggie Benton and offered his assistance.

'Oh, Jake, you are a darling,' she said. 'I think Raymond's supervising the scaffolding team this morning, building the bridge ready for them to bring the marquee across on Wednesday, and we've got to deliver a huge butcher's block to a woman in Mendlesham Green—you couldn't go with Lydia and give her a hand, could you? It's much too heavy for her to lift on her own, and the woman's pregnant.'

Oh, Lord. She was playing into his hands with a vengeance—maybe too much of a vengeance. It was one thing being around, quite another being trapped in the car with her all the way to Mendlesham Green and back. 'Sure,' he agreed, just as Lydia appeared with a tray groaning with coffee and orange juice and a basket of steaming croissants.

'Breakfast,' she said, and plonked it down on the table. 'Now, look, Mum, I really don't think I'm going to be able to do the butcher's block. Can't we get a carrier—?'

'It's all solved,' Maggie said, patting her hand reassuringly. 'Jake's going to help you.'

Her eyes flew up to his, slightly startled, and then an apprehensive smile touched her lips. 'Are you sure?' she said softly, and he felt his last trace of doubt vanish.

'Absolutely. We can't take my car, though; it won't be big enough.'

'Take the Mercedes,' Maggie said matter-of-factly. 'It's all right; Lydia will drive. She only wants your body when you get there.'

He nearly choked on his orange juice, but fortunately she didn't seem to notice and it gave him a moment to recover his composure.

Then he looked up and caught Lydia's unguarded expression. Shock, fascination and—hunger? Then she looked hastily away, soft colour staining her cheeks under the golden tan, and he became aware of the steady pounding of his heart beneath his ribs.

Today was going to be a very interesting day...

CHAPTER THREE

THE butcher's block was, as Maggie had said, huge. After the punishment he'd given his body the day before on the squash court, heaving it in and out of the car brought on a volley of protest from the screaming muscles, but he ignored it, as he ignored the throbbing pain in his head induced by his over-indulgence.

He contented himself with sitting beside Lydia and enjoying the view of her slim, jeans-clad thighs right next to him. He angled himself slightly, so that he could see her without turning his head too much, and watched her as she drove.

She was tense and nervous, either because she hadn't driven in the country for some time, or because he was there. He didn't know which, but she was certainly taut as a bowstring, and after a while she pulled over.

'Could you drive?' she asked.

'Am I insured?'

'Oh, yes, it's insured for anyone over twenty one. I just feel—I don't know, it's been quite a long time since I did it, and I'm not that used to the car. I still feel a bit spaced-out after the travelling, to be honest.'

'Admit it, you're wimping out,' he teased, and she shot him a black look and reached for the keys.

'Forget it,' she said tightly. 'I'll manage.'

He put his hand over hers on the gear lever and stopped her moving it.

'Don't be silly, I was teasing. Of course I'll drive.' He got out of the car, and for a moment he wondered if she was going to drive off and leave him there. He probably deserved it. Oh, damn.

Then her door opened and she emerged, walking round the front as he went round the back, so they didn't even have to pass. Deliberately?

How could he tell—short of asking her? And he wasn't masochist enough to do that. He slid behind the wheel, moved the seat back to accommodate his long legs and checked the mirrors. The seat was warm from her body, and he felt his own react immediately.

Dear God, he was in a bad way! He must be a fool to keep exposing himself to her company like this. Anyone with any sense would have left the country, but not him. Oh, no. He was there, cheerfully volunteering to crawl naked over a bed of hot ashes if it got him nearer to her—

'Oh, hell, you mind, don't you?' she said flatly.

'Mind?'

'Driving.'

He snapped himself out of his ferocious mood and shot her a strained smile.

'Of course I don't. Don't be ridiculous. Can you direct me?'

'Sure. Just keep going straight for now.'

He pulled back on to the road, and she sighed and fidgeted with her seat belt. 'Have you seen Mel today?' she asked after a moment.

'She was with Tom the last time I saw her,' he told

her. 'They didn't look as if they were in a hurry to start the day.'

'Mum will have her guts for garters. They've got the last meeting with the caterer this morning. She'd better be there for that.'

'Ring them on my mobile—tell them to get out of bed. They're probably still there,' he told her, conscious of a pang of envy.

She rang, passed on the message via Tom because Mel was in the shower, and handed him back his phone. 'Thanks,' she murmured, and he grunted and dropped it into his breast pocket and tried not to wish it was him and Lydia in bed, instead of Tom and Mel.

They fell into an uneasy silence, and then after a few minutes he was negotiating the back lanes to the woman's house. Between them they wrestled the heavy carton out of the car and into the kitchen, and unwrapped the butcher's block.

'Oh, it's wonderful!' the woman exclaimed. 'Perfect. It just fills this space—thank you so much, Lydia.'

'My pleasure.' She smiled, and Jake felt his heart kick. She'd smiled at him with that much warmth once, but now her smiles were either sad or reserved, and he ached for one more smile from the bottom of her fickle heart.

She was wimping out of the driving, she knew that, but the car just seemed so big and heavy and the lanes so narrow after the roads in Australia, and she didn't trust herself to negotiate them without putting the car in the ditch.

Anyway, sitting next to him like this gave her a

chance to watch him sneakily, and she found her eyes making frequent sideways trips to linger on the shift of muscles in his powerful thighs, or the flex of his fingers on the steering wheel.

Strong hands—clever hands, hands that had caressed her and made her want much more. Hands she would never feel again.

She looked away, swallowing down the disappointment, and wished once again that she could turn back the clock—

'Fancy stopping for coffee?' he said suddenly, breaking into the endless replay of her regrets.

'Sounds good. There's a place near here, I think, a little tearoom. Will that do?'

'Whatever. I'm not fussy.'

She directed him into the car park at the back of the square in the tiny market town, and they wandered back to the tearoom and sat outside in the sunshine with their coffee, watching the passers-by in a silence that seemed to grow louder by the minute.

'Nice day,' he said after an age, and she laughed without humour.

'We don't seem to know what to say to each other any longer, do we?' she said sadly, and he leant forwards, his spoon dabbling in the coffee, chasing bubbles.

'Did we ever?' he murmured. 'I'm not sure we ever really talked about anything except the house.'

'Maybe that's where we went wrong.'

'Maybe. So what do you want to talk about?'

Why you walked away, she nearly said, but she stopped herself in the nick of time. Anyway she knew the answer. He'd gone because they didn't know each other well enough to be sure of their feelings.

'Whatever,' she said instead with a shrug.

'OK. Tell me about your travels,' he said, settling back against the flimsy little chair and dwarfing it with his broad shoulders.

'Really?' she asked sceptically. 'My time on the hippy trail?'

'You're going to make me pay for that, aren't you?' he said with a rueful smile. 'I really am interested—and I'm sorry I trivialised it and your reasons for going. I was just feeling a little raw. Please tell me.'

So she did, gradually relaxing into it and telling him about the friends she'd made, the things she'd seen and done. She even told him about the man in Delhi who'd tried to rape her, and was startled by the flash of anger in his eyes.

'Were you all right?' he asked with what seemed like genuine concern.

She shrugged, even thinking about the incident making her uneasy. 'Sort of. He didn't really hurt me, but he scared me and made me feel very vulnerable. I'm still not really very comfortable with strange men now.'

'Perhaps you shouldn't be. Perhaps it's a lesson you had to learn. You're a very beautiful and desirable woman, Lydia. I can't be the only man who's noticed.'

She felt warmth suffuse her body. Did he find her desirable? Still, after all that had happened? She looked up and met his eyes, and was stunned by the heat in them. Her tongue flicked out and moistened her suddenly dry lips, and he groaned softly and closed his eyes.

'Go on,' he said gruffly. 'Tell me more about your travels. Tell me about your friends.'

She had to drag her mind back on track. Friends. There were umpteen people she'd met, but only one true friend. 'There was a guy called Leo,' she said slowly. 'I met him in Singapore, and we sort of latched on to each other a bit. We travelled together for a while, and he was very protective. I felt safe with him, but when we got to Australia we split up and he went up north, and I went over to the east coast and worked the holiday season in the Cairns area.'

'Christmas time?' he asked, and she nodded.

'That's right. We were going to meet up for Christmas in Alice Springs, but it just didn't happen. A girl stole all my stuff except my passport and photos, and I had to stay because I didn't have any money for travelling, and then I heard in January that he'd been killed in a road accident. He was driving—moonlighting, of course, because he didn't have a work permit—and he fell asleep at the wheel.'

She went silent, remembering her shock at hearing the news, the terrible sense of loss she'd felt because he was no longer around.

'I'm sorry,' Jake said softly, and she shrugged and tried for a smile, but she suspected it was a pretty poor effort.

'Thanks. Anyway, that was it, really. I went to New Zealand and worked on a sheep farm for a while for a cousin of my father's, and then worked my way back up through Australia doing all sorts of odd cash jobs.'

'It must have been interesting.'

She nodded, remembering it, the good times and the bad, the happy and sad. 'It was. I was ready to come home, though.' Ready for some answers to questions she was almost afraid to ask.

Dangerous territory. Changing the subject swiftly, she glanced at her watch and did a mild double-take. 'Good grief, look at the time! I've been running on for hours. I'm sorry—'

'Don't apologise. For heaven's sake, don't apologise for talking to me—it's long overdue. We should have done this ages ago.'

She met his eyes, and saw genuine regret in them— a regret that matched her own. 'You're right, we never talked enough,' she said quietly.

His hand found hers across the table, his fingers threading through hers with a gentle squeeze. 'We ought to change that. Whatever else happens, we're going to keep seeing each other for years with christenings and the like. We might as well be friends. Think we can manage that?'

Friends. Such a far cry from what she wanted—or was it? Her parents were friends—great friends, best friends. They'd had a wild and stormy relationship at first by all accounts, but it had settled down to deep and abiding friendship and trust.

Maybe friendship wasn't such a bad thing to aim for. At least that way the door between them would stay open and she would get a chance to find out if there was a future for them after this week.

'Yes, I'm sure we can manage it,' she said firmly.

'Good.' He gave her hand one last light squeeze and released it, then stood up. 'We should be heading back. I expect they could use a hand to build the bridge over the river.'

'Probably. I expect I'll end up running errands for Mum again if we go home, but I suppose I can always volunteer myself for bridge-building, too.'

In fact the bridge was built, but they went down to admire it and look at the field where the cars would park on Saturday.

'If it only stays dry, we should be all right,' Raymond Benton said, studying the sky as if to read the answer.

'If it rains, they'll have to park on the top field,' Lydia said philosophically. 'It's not insurmountable.'

'No.' He hugged her to his side, and shot Jake a quizzical look. 'You seen that friend of yours today? He seems to have hijacked our other daughter.'

Jake gave a wry smile. 'Has he? Sensible fellow. I haven't seen them since this morning, I'm afraid.' Sprawled together in sensual abandon and showing no signs of getting up, although they'd promised to go to the meeting with the caterers. He wondered if they'd just had enough of all the wedding fuss, and wasn't surprised.

'Oh, well, I dare say they'll turn up,' Raymond was saying. 'Lydia, darling, the florists are due here in half an hour for the last check-through. Could you give your mother a hand? Mel's already missed the caterers.'

'Sure,' she agreed, and, hugging him briefly, she turned to Jake. 'Shall we grab some lunch?'

'Sounds good,' he said, wondering how long their truce could last and if they'd fall out again before the end of the week. Not that they'd exactly fallen out before, just—what? Failed to communicate?

In a major way! He followed her up to the house and into the kitchen, and there they found Mel and Tom being lovingly chastised by Maggie.

'Where were you, for heaven's sake? You are so naughty,' she scolded, and Mel kissed her mother and smiled that thousand-watt smile and was instantly forgiven. Jake caught Tom's eye and raised a brow, and Tom winked.

Rascal. Jake felt the smile fade from his face, replaced by a look that he feared might be altogether too revealing.

'Anything I can do?' he asked to fill the gap, and Maggie pounced on him.

'Jake, you're a darling. Unwrap the cheese. It's a simple lunch, I'm afraid, just cheese and biscuits and fruit and mineral water. Melanie, plates, darling, please, and Tom, can you carry the table round to the terrace and put the benches out? There's a love. Lydia, wash the fruit for me, could you, sweetheart?'

And just like that they were all dispatched, coming together moments later to eat their meal with Raymond, who came up from the bottom of the garden in answer to Maggie's call.

As they ate, they talked through the last-minute arrangements, and Jake got an uncomfortable sense of *déjà vu*. Lydia, too, seemed uneasy, and it was almost with relief that the meal was cleared away and they were free to escape.

'Now, Lydia, you're going to have to see the dress-

maker this afternoon and have that dress taken in,'
Maggie said as they took everything into the kitchen.
'It just hangs at the moment. Oh, and while you're
there, could you pick up my hat? She was putting a
band on it to match the dress.'

'Sure,' Lydia agreed. 'Where is she?'

'Woodbridge—you know the woman.'

Her face fell, and Jake wondered how much harder
it could get for her. Had none of them thought of the
consequences of using last year's plan, last year's caterers and florists, last year's marquee, last year's
dressmaker?

'I'll take you,' he found himself saying, and she
shot him a grateful look.

'Would you? I'm not sure I can remember the
way.'

'Sure. Let's go.'

'Oh, I need to ring her,' Maggie said, stopping their
retreat. 'Hang on—oh, damn, the flower people are
here.'

'We'll chance it,' Lydia said hastily, and bolted out
of the door.

Jake followed her, murmuring thanks for their
lunch, and caught up with her as she headed up the
drive.

'Shall we take your car?' she suggested, her hands
wrapped round and hugging her arms to her chest.
She looked tense and unhappy and he wanted to hug
her.

'OK. We can take a stroll by the river when you're
done, if you like.'

She nodded distractedly, and out of sight of the
others he slung an affectionate arm around her shoul-

ders and tried to keep his libido under control. 'Hey, it's going to be all right, Lydia. It's just a dress.'

'She's such a nosy woman—she's got an opinion on everything. She's bound to mention last year.'

'Just tell her I dumped you.'

She shot him a horrified look. 'What, and have all that sympathy? You have to be joking.'

'So tell her you took a raincheck. Tell her it's pending.'

'After what Mel will have told her?' she asked sceptically. 'They're as bad as each other. I should think every intimate detail of my life's been gone over with a fine-tooth comb.'

Oh, hell. He gave her shoulder a quick squeeze and let her go, because he was just too comfortable with her tucked under his arm and it could easily become a habit.

'Just keep it brief. I'll come in with you—'

'No!' she exclaimed, horrified. 'That will just make it worse! I'll deal with her. I'll tell her I wanted to see the world before I settled down.'

Did that mean, Jake wondered, that she was now ready to settle down? Or was it just something to tell a nosy and interfering busybody? He had no idea. He waited outside for her, trying not to think about the late, lamented Leo and what kind of a relationship they might have had, and after what seemed like an age she emerged, walking backwards down the path with the woman still talking nineteen to the dozen.

'I'll pick it up on Wednesday,' she promised, putting a huge hat box in the back seat, and dived into the car, slamming the door and giving a little wave.

'Quick. Drive off before she thinks of anything else to say.'

'Did she give you the third degree?'

She dropped her head back against the seat and sighed hugely. 'Did she ever. I had to tell her about everything I did in the last year, and I got a lecture on not eating and being too thin—'

'Quite right too,' Jake murmured, throwing her a smile. 'You could do with a few square meals.'

'What, like that breakfast?' she said with a grin. 'I couldn't do that every day.'

You could have done, he thought with a touch of sadness. You could have, every weekend for the last year—

'How about tea?' he suggested casually. 'There must be somewhere on the river.'

They found a little café and had tea, and shared a huge slice of chocolate cake.

Well, they had a plate and two forks, and Jake toyed with it and Lydia dived into it head-first and came up with a wry grin a few minutes later.

'That was luscious,' she said, and he laughed.

'Good.'

'I mustn't do it too often; the dress will be too tight,' she said with a sigh. 'As it is I might have to send you to fetch it. I don't think I can face her again.'

'Nice try, but you know she'll demand a fitting, and as sure as eggs it won't fit me,' he said drily, and she chuckled.

'Yes, you're right, and anyway she'd grill you till you told her what you'd been up to for the last year.'

'That wouldn't take many seconds,' he replied. He

felt his smile slip and put the cup down in the saucer with a little clunk. 'Shall we go? I've just remembered I've got to make a call.'

She gave him a curious look, but shrugged and put her tea down unfinished. 'OK. Whatever. I'm sorry, I seem to have taken up hours of your time and you probably ought to be busy.'

He wanted to correct her, but he felt edgy suddenly, and vulnerable. Threatened. Exposed. Raw.

He didn't want to think about the last year. It had been cold and lonely and dark without her, and he'd thrown himself into his work rather than have time to wonder just which aspect of his character she'd found so unpalatable.

He had to force himself not to stride away from her but to go at a normal pace along the riverside walk that led to the car park. She walked beside him in silence, probably too busy keeping up to talk, and he felt another pang of guilt and slowed down.

This whole week seemed to be inducing pangs of guilt, and he was slightly at a loss to know why he, of the two of them, should be feeling guilty, but he was.

Maybe because he, of course, was the one with the ulterior motive. For some reason best known to his subconscious, he was deliberately seeking out her company, although God knows this was going nowhere.

Once they were back in the car and under way, he forced his shoulders to relax and took a long, deep breath.

'I'm sorry,' she said quietly, and he turned and looked at her in surprise.

'Sorry?'

'It's just as difficult for you—maybe harder. I keep dragging you along on all these errands—wouldn't you rather just go to London and come back on Saturday?'

Ten seconds ago, maybe, he would have agreed with her, but there was something about the look in her eyes that stopped him.

'It's fine. Don't worry yourself about me, I'm a big boy, Lydia. What about you?'

She laughed softly, her shoulders lifting in an expressive little shrug. 'Oh, I'm a big boy too, so to speak, but it's still—awkward. There have been times when I wish I'd stayed in Australia a bit longer.'

'I'll buy that,' he muttered, and then, without letting himself stop to think, he went on, 'Look, there's a party I've been invited to—an old schoolfriend's thirtieth. It's on Wednesday night, in Ealing. I thought I'd go down—stay at the flat, go to the party for a couple of hours, perhaps drop into the office on Thursday on the way back. Why don't you come with me?'

Her alarm was screaming, but strangely she'd gone deaf to it. A night in London, partying and getting away from it all generally, sounded wonderful.

'Thanks. If you really mean it, I will,' she said with a slightly hesitant smile.

'Of course I mean it,' he said, and for a moment she wondered if he was trying to convince himself or if, like the breakfast invitation, he'd regret extending it.

They were heading back through the gently rolling

countryside when they passed a sign pointing to a field.

'Strawberries!' she said. 'Jake, let's go and pick strawberries! It's a pick-your-own place—you pick half and eat half, and I haven't had strawberries for a year. Please?'

He looked into her beseeching eyes and was lost.

'OK,' he said, pulling up and turning the car round. 'The lady wants strawberries; the lady can have strawberries.'

She flashed him a mega-watt smile, and he felt the impact of that smile all the way down to his boots.

Fruit-picking wasn't something new to Lydia. She'd done more of it in New Zealand than she cared to think about, but not English strawberries. Somehow they just tasted different, and her mouth watered as they headed towards the rows of little plants nodding with huge, juicy fruit.

'Oh, wow,' she said, dropping to her knees and choosing the biggest, ripest one she could find. She bit into it and the juice ran down her chin, and she laughed and licked the juice off and held one up to Jake.

'Here—eat it. They're gorgeous.'

For a moment he hesitated, then he bent and put his even white teeth around the fruit and tugged gently.

'Isn't it gorgeous?' she prompted, and he gave a slow, lazy smile and swallowed.

'Oh, yes—but I question whether we're supposed to eat them instead of picking them.'

She flapped a hand and laughed. 'Everyone does it.

It's built in to the pricing system—but my mother always said they should have weighed me on the way in and the way out, and charged us the difference!'

He chuckled and crouched beside her in the next row, working his way through the plants with a selective and discerning eye. Every now and then he'd allow himself one, but Lydia worked on a 'one for me, two for the punnet' principle, and when his punnet was full hers was only halfway there, because of course she'd had to pause to savour them.

'She said there are some raspberries, too,' Lydia said hopefully, and he gave her an indulgent smile and straightened up.

'Come on, then, let's get another punnet for them.'

The raspberries were, if anything, even juicier. Lydia popped one in her mouth and closed her eyes, groaning in ecstasy. 'Oh, they are the best—here, try,' she insisted, and put one between his parted lips.

Their eyes locked, and for a moment he stood there, the fruit caught between his teeth, and her heart lurched in her chest.

Then he looked away, turning his attention to the raspberry canes, his shoulder brushing hers as he worked his way through the bush in silence.

Then they reached for the same raspberry, and her fingers closed over it a second before his. Gently he tugged, and the fruit came away in her hand, and he lifted it to his mouth and took it from her fingers.

She felt the shock of the contact all the way to her toes. He took the raspberry into his mouth, and his lips pressed against her fingers in the softest kiss. Then he dropped his hand and straightened up.

'I think we've got enough,' he said in a voice that sounded rusty and unused.

She looked down into the punnet, only half full, and belatedly remembered he was supposed to be making a call. And she'd distracted him again for her own ends. When would she learn not to be so selfish?

'I'm sorry, you said you'd got to get back ages ago. What am I thinking about?'

He looked puzzled for a fleeting second, then murmured something non-committal and headed back towards the weigh-in point.

'Oh, look—redcurrants!' she said as the girl weighed their fruit.

'Yes—they're very early this year. We don't usually get any before July, but it's been so warm for so long. We've got a few blackcurrants, too.'

Lydia turned to Jake. 'We could have summer pudding,' she said in delight. 'Oh, yes, we must have some. Can we have one of each, please?'

And then, of course, when it was all totted up Jake insisted on paying, and with a wry grin asked the girl to add on the cost of half a pound of strawberries—'for tasting purposes,' he said. And she laughed breathlessly and said no, it was all right, it was part of the deal, and Lydia thought she was going to faint on the fruit.

Poor girl. He'd always had that effect on women, she thought wryly. Her mother was under his spell well and truly, and she'd felt the same when she'd first met him and thought he was the most amazing and wonderful person she'd ever come across in her entire life...

CHAPTER FOUR

SHE was sitting on the bench outside the kitchen window, with her skirt hitched up to the top of her thighs and her bare legs stretched out to the April sun, the first time she met him.

He came down the drive and she heard footsteps in the gravel, crisp and decisive, and thought it must be one of the men from the kitchen workshop looking for her mother, or one of the farm hands coming down to the farm office for a coffee break.

Whatever, Molly didn't growl and she could hear the steady beat of the dog's tail, so she ignored the footsteps until a shadow fell across her, blocking out the sun from her legs. Then she sat up, her eyes screwed up so she could see him outlined against the sun, and her heart tripped instantly.

This was no one she knew, no one she'd ever met before. If she had, she would have remembered.

She couldn't make out his features, but there was something about him that made her immediately and totally aware of him. She shifted her head, screening her eyes with her hand, and finally she could see him properly.

He was gorgeous—tall, well-built but not heavy, his dark hair soft and thick, short enough to be tidy but long enough to run your fingers through. He was dressed in casual trousers, shirt undone at the neck, jacket slung over his shoulder on one finger, and he smiled at her and the world tilted on its axis.

Suddenly remembering her state of undress, she hastily dragged her skirt down over her knees and stood up, hoping he'd put the heat in her cheeks down to the sun and not his sudden appearance in her line of sight.

'Um—hi,' she said, her mouth tilting into a smile without her permission. 'Sorry, I was miles away. Can I help you?'

'I'm your new neighbour—I thought I'd drop by and introduce myself. I'm Jake Delaney.' He held out his hand and smiled, and she wondered if he was laughing at her or if his eyes always twinkled like that.

'Nice to meet you. I'm Lydia,' she replied automatically, awestruck by his sheer physical presence and stunned by the amazing blue of those twinkling eyes. 'Lydia Benton—hello. Welcome to the area.' Dredging up a smile she hoped wasn't too inane, she took his hand, and tingles ran up her arm and settled in her heart, shooting her pulse-rate up to the danger zone.

She retrieved her hand before he realised what a mental case she'd turned into, and groped for common sense. 'Um—my father's out on the farm at the moment, I think, but Mum's about. Come on in—can I get you a drink?'

He smiled again, his mouth kicking up at the corners and once more playing hell with her heart-rate. 'That would be lovely. A coffee, perhaps?'

'Sure. Come into the kitchen. I'll call Mum; she's probably in the study.'

He followed her in, casually dropping his jacket over the back of a chair and bending to pat the dog, and she put the kettle on the Aga and stuck her head through the kitchen door. Her mother was just coming out of the study.

'Did I hear voices?' she asked with a smile, and Lydia nodded.

'Yes, our new neighbour. He's in the kitchen. I was just going to make coffee for us all.'

'Oh, lovely.' She went through and held out her hand. 'Maggie Benton. Welcome to the village.'

'Thank you, I'm Jake Delaney.' He shook her hand, and her mother smiled approvingly. She liked a firm handshake, Lydia remembered, and Jake's was firm.

Jake's was all sorts of other things, too, but she wouldn't dwell on that now or she'd pour boiling water all over herself.

She made coffee in the cafetière, and they settled round the table, with Molly leaning adoringly on his leg, and Jake told them all about his purchase.

Well, to be exact, Maggie asked and prompted and wheedled and Jake had no option but to tell all. Her mother was an expert at getting people to yield up their secrets.

Lydia didn't mind at all. She was perfectly content just sitting listening to the sound of his voice and hearing all about how he'd come to find the house.

'It's a tip, of course,' he said with a wry grin. 'It's practically derelict.'

'Oh, I know,' Maggie said. 'The old boy who lived there did nothing for the last couple of years, and precious little before that, but at least you aren't having to rip out new fittings that just aren't in keeping or to your taste.'

He chuckled, those blue eyes flashing and sparkling and doing terrible things to her blood pressure. 'There's nothing to rip out, believe me. The kitchen's just a couple of thirties cupboards with white enamel tops on, and a terrible cream enamelled sink with chips and dents. Nothing worth worrying about at all.'

He looked around and sighed. 'This, on the other hand, is beautiful. Have you had it done by a local firm?'

Maggie laughed softly. 'In a manner of speaking.'

'What Mum means,' Lydia chipped in, 'is that she wanted to get it refitted and couldn't find anyone locally who could do the job to her satisfaction. She wasn't prepared to spend the cost of a small house having it refitted, so she employed some cabinet makers and did it herself, and it was so successful she set up a company.'

Jake's ears seemed to prick. 'Really? So when I come to do my kitchen—'

'We'd be delighted to give you a quote,' Maggie said with a mischievous smile. 'Are you moving in now?'

He laughed, a low, husky sound that was music to Lydia's ears. 'Not quite. It needs a few basic facilities before I can live in it, but it's mine now, anyway, so I can allow myself to plan a bit. Fancy a look?'

Maggie glanced at her watch, and sighed. 'I'd love to, but I'm busy; I've got a client coming. What a shame—but Lydia could, couldn't you, darling? You could do a preliminary survey and scribble down a few ideas.'

Client? Lydia thought. It was news to her, but she wasn't going to pass up an opportunity to see the house, *or* spend time with him! She shrugged. 'Sure. I was supposed to be out on site this morning but they had to cancel, so I'm at loose end—hence I was sitting in the sun. Yes, if you like and you've got time I can come over and have a look now.'

His smile widened. 'Excellent. I had no idea it could be so easy. I've been looking at adverts in glossies and wondering what to do, but they're so remote, these big firms, and I'd rather use local labour anyway. Talking of which, I don't suppose you've got a builder or a plumber in your pocket?'

Maggie laughed. 'Actually, I have both—we work closely alongside all the associated trades. Lydia can give you their numbers, can't you, darling? I'm sorry, I'm going to have to fly. I'm still working on the quote for this client. I'll see you later. It's lovely to meet you, Jake.'

And so, without any time to worry about what she was wearing and if she looked respectable enough or professional enough or just plain *clean* enough, never mind feminine or desirable, she found herself walking up the road beside the best-looking man she'd ever met in her life, utterly riveted by his easy charm and the clear, deep blue of those wonderful eyes.

As they approached the house, Lydia ran her eyes appreciatively over the mellow red bricks, the tall white sash windows, the delicate fanlight over the front door. The house had a pleasing symmetry, and because of the reclusive owner and the air of secrecy that hung about it, it had always fascinated her. Now, as she was about to enter it for the first time, she felt a quiver of excitement and anticipation.

'Sorry, it's a real tip,' he said with an apologetic smile as he opened the blistered and peeling door and pushed a stack of junk mail out of the way. 'Come on in—and for goodness' sake, tell me it wasn't all a dreadful mistake!'

'Mistake?' she laughed, enchanted. 'It's lovely! Oh, look, it's got a proper chequer-pattern floor in encaustic tiles—look, here, can you see it? Oh, that's wonderful!'

She bent, pushing aside the junk mail, and showed him the pretty red and blue and cream tiles, bordered in a twisted helix pattern of red on cream, very traditional for country houses of the period. 'Oh, you are lucky. Ours was so badly trashed we had to take it up, and there was only enough to put it down in the downstairs loo. Still, at least we managed to rescue a bit!'

She straightened up and looked round, taking in the rest of the hall with a sigh of delight. The lovely sweeping stairs rose gracefully from one side of the hall, with a solid mahogany banister rail that ended at the bottom with an architectural curl instead of a newel post, and a cluster of broken balusters doing a half-hearted job of supporting it. It was encrusted with dirt and grease but original and untouched—even to the point of the balusters that had never been repaired.

The doors all stood open, and she could see into what had once been a fine drawing room and was now just a junk heap. The other doors revealed a similar story, and she shook her head in amazement.

'I never realised it was this bad,' she murmured.

'I'm surprised you didn't ever come in.'

She flicked her eyes up to his and laughed softly. 'Oh, no. He was a total recluse. He hated absolutely everybody—he wouldn't even let the district nurse in. He certainly didn't want to get to know his neighbours.'

'What a wasted opportunity,' Jake said with a slow smile. 'Come and see the kitchen.'

'Can I see the rest of the house first?' she asked, back to business. 'It helps to know what you're trying to fit in with. Do you have any idea what sort of feel you're going for?'

'Feel?' he said with a chuckle. 'Try clean. Try mended!'

She laughed again, and looked at the stairs suspiciously. 'I take it they are safe? Only I'm very cautious since I saw that film *The Money Pit* with Tom Hanks, where the staircase collapses.'

Jake chuckled. 'I think we're OK on the stairs, but the plumbing might have a lot in common. Remember the gloop in the bath?'

Lydia shuddered and laughed. 'Come on, then, if it's safe. Let's have a look round and talk through what sort of period feel you're going for. It helps me to get the kitchen right—I assume you do want the kitchen to fit in with the period of the house and not be ultra-modern and high-tech?'

He shook his head. 'No. I've got high-tech in London. I want something different here—something country and solid and dependable. Something as old as the hills and with a bit of weight to it.'

She nodded in agreement, and after a quick tour of the house, all rather sad and tired but essentially beautiful, they went down to the kitchen and stood in the middle of the big, soulless room and stared in silence.

'Hmm,' she said softly, and he chuckled.

'Quite so. I think characterless is perhaps too strong a word.'

'Well, it certainly won't win any awards,' she agreed, checking out the chimney positioning, the doors and windows, the general dimensions with a practised eye. 'Still, it's a good basic shape. Tell me what you want from it while I measure up.'

He told her, with prompting, and then they went back to her own family kitchen and sat round the big table with loads of pictures and sketches and ideas, and then she stopped.

'You need to think about it for a while,' she told him. 'You can't make quick decisions. I'll throw a few ideas together for you and you can look at them next time you're up, if you like?'

'Could you post them?' he asked, and she felt a sudden strange reluctance to do so. For some reason that she wasn't really ready to examine, she wanted to go through it personally.

'Then I could come up and talk it through with you when I've had time to think about it,' he went on, and a little surge of relief rippled through her.

'That would be fine. You'd better give me your address.'

He handed her a card, just a simple crisp white card with black writing, nothing flashy about it—except the address, in a highly exclusive neighbourhood near Butler's Wharf. It was probably one of those fantastic converted lofts with a view over the Thames, she thought numbly, and nodded.

'OK. That's fine. It'll take me a few days.'

He smiled, and it warmed her right through. 'I'll be waiting with bated breath.'

It took her two days, and he rang her the evening after she posted it.

'Thanks for the designs,' he began. 'I was wondering how busy you are tomorrow. I have to come up to see the builder—I wondered if we could talk about the kitchen over lunch, perhaps?'

She was busy. Tough, she decided, and spent the rest of the evening doing a massive rescheduling of her day's meetings and commitments to free her up for lunch and the rest of the afternoon.

Surprisingly her mother was highly co-operative. 'He's an important client. Not only is it a big and commercially valuable job, he's going to be living next to us for however long. We all need to live with the consequences of these decisions, so they'd better be right.'

And so, with her mother's blessing, she went out for lunch with Jake Delaney, her heart dancing and skittering around in her throat and her mind struggling to concentrate on anything but those dreamy, sexy, stunningly blue eyes and his slow, lazy smile.

They went to the pub in the village and sat outside at one of the picnic benches under a tree, with the sound of the river in the background and the breeze fluttering the pages. They thrashed through her ideas and his and sketched out a couple of possibles while they munched their way through juicy prawn salad sandwiches and drank gallons of iced water with crisp wedges of lemon and lime.

Finally he straightened up. 'Let's go back to the

house and look at the ideas *in situ*, can we? Do you have enough time?'

'I've made time,' she told him with a smile. 'I had a feeling it would take a while, and if it didn't, I wanted to have time to get it all down on paper before I forgot. Don't you have to see the builder, though?'

'I've done it—we met at ten o'clock. I'm all yours for the rest of the day.'

His smile did crazy things to her insides, but by a massive effort of will she managed not to throw herself at him. She settled for a grin that seemed to stretch from ear to ear.

'Let's go, then,' she said, and he escorted her to the car, opening the door and settling her like a maiden aunt—or someone very special. Not that he'd given her any hint that she was special to him, so she could only assume he'd been practising on the maiden aunt!

'So how did you get on with the builder?' she asked on the short drive back, and he shrugged.

'He was a prophet of doom. They always are. Not given to looking on the bright side, but then I knew that. I've dealt with builders before and they're all tarred with the same brush. Lots of, "Ooh, well, of course we could do that, but it'll be expensive," and masses of face-pulling and head-scratching and the like, but at the end of the day he seemed very sensible.'

'He is,' Lydia assured him, struggling to hide her smile. 'Mum always says he's miserable, but he does a fantastic job. You just have to take the pessimism with a pinch of salt, and he only ever charges you what he's quoted for the job.'

'That makes a change, then,' he said with a chuckle, and turned onto his drive. 'Right, let's go and see the real thing and find out why it won't work.'

'Oh, ye of little faith,' Lydia laughed. 'I surveyed it, remember? It'll be fine.'

To her great relief it was, and they planned the last tiny details while she made copious notes, and then he met her eyes over the barren and dreadful kitchen and smiled a smile that nearly melted the soles of her shoes.

'I'm so grateful,' he said softly. 'I really thought it was going to be the most awful hassle, and you've made it almost fun.'

'You haven't got the quote yet,' she warned with a laugh, but he brushed it aside.

'I'm sure it will be fine. Even if it's not, I still want you to do it. We seem to be on the same wavelength, and I want to like it.'

'You won't be ripped off,' she promised, and he smiled again, just when her heart had settled down.

'I know. You're all much too honest, and anyway, we'll be neighbours. I'm not optimistic enough to expect special treatment, but I'm damn sure you'll make certain it's not a disaster.'

She thought of her mother's words the night before and hid a smile. How true, she thought, and wondered how long she could drag on the planning and meetings stage without giving herself away.

'When are you coming back?' she asked, and hoped she didn't sound too wistful.

'The weekend, maybe. I've got to fly to New York tomorrow on business, and I won't be back till Friday. Is that OK, or are weekends sacred?'

She laughed. 'My father's a farmer. Weekends are just another couple of days in the week. Don't worry about it.'

'I'll ring you when I get back, then.' He glanced at his watch and pulled a face. 'I don't suppose there's any chance of a cup of tea before I head off back to town, is there?'

A little shiver danced along her veins, and she gathered up all her papers with a smile. 'Of course. If we're really lucky there'll be some of Mel's fruitcake left. It's the best.'

So they sat for another hour, drinking endless cups of tea and finishing off the rich, moist cake, and then her mother came in and suggested he should stay for supper, and it was nearly nine before he finally stood up to go.

She walked him to his car, promising to have something more concrete for him to look at by the weekend, and then after an endless pause, when the air was electric and she hoped wildly that he would kiss her, one eye drooped in a sexy wink and he slid behind the wheel and drove slowly away.

She went back into the kitchen, and there, lined up facing her like a firing squad, were her family, their eyes alight with fascination and curiosity. As if he'd really kissed her, instead of just her wishful thinking, she coloured softly, and then, of course, she had to sit through their good-natured ribbing.

'He's gorgeous,' Mel began, the words sounding like a question.

'When are you seeing him again?' her mother asked with studied uninterest.

'The weekend—he wants to see the plans—'

Mel's rude noise interrupted her flow, and she shot her younger sister a quelling look. 'He's a client,' she explained patiently, but Mel wasn't listening. Clever girl that she was, she sliced straight through all the professional interest rubbish and cut to the chase.

'He's gorgeous, and he fancies you, and you aren't telling me it's not mutual or that he'd be just as interested in his boring old kitchen if you were a man.'

Colour warmed her cheeks again, and she looked away, straight into the searching eyes of her mother.

'You could do worse,' she said with a smile, and Lydia wanted to scream at them and deny it, but of course she couldn't, because every word of it was true.

'I don't want to complicate things,' she said honestly, and her father, quiet until then, gave a low chuckle.

'It's the sort of complication that makes the world go round, my darling,' he said contentedly. 'I thought he seemed very pleasant. I suppose he does have enough money to pay for the kitchen?'

Lydia laughed out loud. 'Oh, I think so. He lives near Butler's Wharf, probably in one of those fabulous loft things. He said it was very high-tech. I suspect he's not short of money.'

'Make sure he knows that we won't stitch him on the quote just because he can afford it,' Maggie said, 'bearing in mind he is a neighbour.'

'She's more likely to undercharge him to earn Brownie points,' Mel said drily.

'Rubbish. I'll price it accurately,' Lydia told them all. 'He's a client first and foremost. What you decide to do about discounts and delivery times is up to you.

I'm just the designer—and I've got designing to do before I forget what he said.'

Mel snorted again. 'Not a chance. Every word that man's said to you is engraved on your memory.'

It was, but there was no way she was admitting it. She made herself a cup of coffee and went into the study, set up the drawing board and committed all their designs to paper.

They didn't use CAD—a computer-aided design seemed too impersonal for the sort of work they did. Instead Lydia, with her training as an interior designer, did the drawings and prepared the coloured visuals, and they only used the computer to show a client quickly how various options might look.

Once they'd settled on something, it was always drawn up by Lydia again, to incorporate all the fine tuning and detail that the computer couldn't generate.

For Jake, though, Lydia intended to do visuals of the options as well, even if it meant she had to stay up all night in order to find the time!

'Wow.'

Pleasure flooded her at his reaction, and she couldn't help but smile. 'You like it?'

'I love it. I can't wait. When will you start?'

She shrugged. 'A few weeks? The builder needs to strip everything out and replaster it once the outside's weathertight, and the pamment floor in there and the butler's pantry need relaying and the windows need repair, so while that's happening we can get the units made up ready to slot straight in. Because you're having quite a lot of free-standing things, it won't be such a hassle to install it, but the big dresser wall will take a while to fit together and that'll have to be done on site.'

'So when can you start making the units?'

She smiled at his impatience. 'Next week? The week after? We're in a bit of a lull at the moment, so you're lucky. How about the quote, though? Don't you even want to ask?'

He laughed softly. 'I told you about that.'

Lydia gave a slow smile and slid a pile of paper across the kitchen table towards him. 'Well, just so you know you haven't been stitched up, here's the final figure. The breakdown is underneath it.'

She held her breath, waiting for him to flinch because it was an involved and quite tricky job in a way, and would take a lot of man-hours and materials, but he simply scanned it and nodded.

'It's fine. Are you sure it's enough?'

She felt the tension drain out of her, and realised she'd been holding her breath. 'It's enough. It's fair and it's accurate, as far as I can tell. There may be the odd change as we go along, but we'll negotiate them as and when they arise. We won't rip you off on extras, Jake.'

'I know.' He gave a wry smile. 'Can we go and see it again? See the plans in the context of reality?'

'Sure.'

They walked round to his house, plans in hand, and the light breeze was fresh and sweet with the scent of blossom. It was a glorious day, and Lydia wanted to dance and sing with happiness, because he was back from America and liked her quote and her drawings and he was just *there* again.

They went into the kitchen and talked it through

for the umpteenth time, and then he put the plans down and looked deep into her eyes, and her heart nearly stopped.

'We ought to shake on it, really,' he murmured, 'but that seems a bit formal somehow.'

'It does?' she said breathlessly.

'Mmm-hmm.' His mouth kicked up in a lop-sided smile. 'Anyway, I have a better idea.' And he drew her gently into his arms, lowered his head and kissed her.

Stunned, she stood there in his arms without moving, and then after a moment he straightened. 'Lydia?' he murmured, and it seemed to break the spell and set her free.

Her hands came up and cupped the back of his head, and she drew him down again and kissed him back, just once, just lightly.

'I take it that's a deal, then?' he said in a slightly strangled voice, and she laughed softly and stepped back out of the temptation of his arms.

'I think so. I think we can work together, don't you?'

His eyes tracked over her and his mouth flickered in a slight and curiously intimate smile. 'Oh, yes,' he said softly. 'I think so.'

'That's good, then,' she said a little breathlessly, gathering up all her papers and plans and drawings and handing them to him. 'Here, these are your copies. I would have bound them for you in a ring binder but I ran out of time.'

'I'll get it done at the office,' he said dismissively, putting them down again on one of the battered enamel worktops. 'So what happens now?'

Now? she thought. Now? What about now? For a moment she couldn't think what he meant, and a shiver of terrified anticipation ran through her veins. 'Now?' she all but squeaked.

'Yes—about the kitchen. Do I give you a deposit? Do you want me to pay up-front, or stage it, or do you want credit references, or cash or what?'

Relief and disappointment coursed through her. 'Oh. Um—you need to talk to my mother. I think probably stage payments would make sense, because the bleached oak is very expensive, but she'll draw up an order and send it to you to sign before we go any further. That'll give you a cooling-off period.'

'I don't need a cooling-off period,' he murmured, and she felt all hot and cold again.

'Whatever, that's how she does it. Shall we go and break the news?'

'If you like,' he said, shrugging away from the wall with a slow smile. 'Or we could go out somewhere and have lunch—unless you're busy?'

She wasn't busy, of course, except in that she had work left over that she'd put on one side that really, really needed doing before Monday. But there was the rest of the weekend—

'Lunch would be lovely,' she said with a smile, and wondered if her heartbeat was actually visible through the soft cotton of her shirt…

Progress on the kitchen was slow, and Jake was away a great deal for the next two weeks. By the time he came back the builder was in, and the cosy intimacy of the room was lost.

So they moved, instead, to the rest of the house to plan and plot its restoration.

'You need a new conservatory,' she said, standing in what ought to have been the breakfast or morning room. It faced east, and on its southern side were the remains of a conservatory, long crumbled away.

'Not as much as I need a kiss,' he murmured, and drew her into his arms. 'I've missed you. Hong Kong was dull without you.'

'I'm sure it wasn't,' she laughed, but he cut her off with his hand placed lightly over her mouth.

'Oh, it was,' he assured her, just as his head lowered. His mouth replaced his hand, as he took her lips in a gentle but unbelievably powerful kiss that left her shaken and trembling.

After a moment he lifted his head and looked down at her, and his eyes were dark and full of promise. 'That's better,' he murmured, and his mouth claimed hers again. 'Much better.'

He took her to 'their' pub for lunch, and they sat in the garden under a tree and leant against the trunk at right angles to each other as he told her about Hong Kong and what he'd been doing there. She found herself asking him questions about his company—and then discovered it was actually companies, that he was an engineer and bought up small firms with promise that were struggling, and helped them find their niche in the market.

It was obviously worth while, if his address in London and his profligate attitude to his kitchen quote were anything to go by.

Teasingly, she accused him of asset-stripping, and

he lost his smile and assured her that he never, ever stripped the assets of a company and dumped it—not unless the people running it were crooked and deserved it, in which case he bought them off and did his best for the rest of their workforce.

'I'll have to call you Robin Hood if you tell me much more,' she teased, and he gave a wry laugh and pulled her into the crook of his arm.

'Are you winding me up?' he asked mildly, and she laughed softly and kissed him.

'Would I?'

'Very likely. Come on, drink up. I want to talk through some ideas I've got for the rest of the house.'

They went back, and she listened with interest, commenting on everything because she was just like that, and then, when they went into what would be his bedroom, he leant against the wall, folded his arms and said, 'Tell me what you'd do in here.'

Love you, she thought, and then gathered her scattered wits and looked around. It was a beautiful room, with two long windows overlooking the garden, and she imagined lying in a great high bed and looking out across the garden towards the river.

'It needs a four-poster,' she said slowly. 'A huge mahogany one, with slender, barley-twist posts with carved bases, and a great carved headboard, and I'd do it all cream to set off the gleaming wood. No pattern—or at least only very pale, like a toile de Jouy or something like that.'

She was getting into it now, and waved her arms as she described the fullness of the curtains and the drape of them behind the bed, and then he took her into the dressing room off it and said he was thinking of creating an *en suite* bathroom.

'Oh, fantastic—it's huge! You could have one of those fabulous Victorian showers with brass pipes all round with heads on that give you a total body shower—they use gallons of water, but they're wonderful. And a roll-top bath with ball and claw feet and huge brass taps coming up from the floor, and an old loo and a basin set into a washstand—you'll have to go to a reclamation yard to get everything, of course.'

'And of course you know just the place.'

She flashed him a sparkling smile. 'Of course. We use it all the time. Want to go?'

He laughed softly. 'Yes, but not now. Now I want to kiss you again. Come here, Princess.'

So she went into his arms, and he kissed her until her knees buckled, then he turned her so she was leaning against the wall and pressed one solid, firm thigh between hers to prop her up, and kissed her again, and again, until his breath was ragged and his chest was heaving and she could hear the thunder of his heart over the roar of her own.

'Do you have any idea,' he said unsteadily into her hair, 'just what you do to me?'

Her hands were gripping his shirt, and she released it and flattened her palms against the strong column of his spine, stroking it soothingly. 'A fair idea. I imagine it's closely related to what you do to me.'

He lifted his head and looked down into her face, and the raw hunger in his eyes shocked and thrilled her. 'If that four-poster bed was there, you'd be in it,' he vowed, and desire ripped through her again, taking her breath in a tiny gasp of need.

'Don't do that, Princess,' he pleaded. 'Don't make it any more difficult. There's a builder in the house, so you're safe—for the moment. But don't push it—not unless you're going all the way.'

Right on cue, the hammering stopped, and they could hear voices in the hall.

'Mr Delaney?' the builder called. 'Plumber's here to talk to you.'

'Coming,' he called. 'Damn nearly, anyway,' he added softly for her benefit, and she gave a strangled little laugh. With a sigh he moved away, withdrawing the support of his body so that she nearly fell, and she flattened her hands against the wall to stop herself sliding down it and landing in a puddle at his feet.

'I think you've done something to my legs,' she grumbled, and he gave a rueful smile.

'Think of me. I have to go and talk to a plumber, and my mind is definitely going to be elsewhere.'

He walked away, and she stayed there for a moment, gathering her scattered thoughts. She'd had no idea a mere kiss could do that to a person, and her body was humming and singing in ways she had hitherto only imagined.

She laughed. She'd been way off beam. Nothing in her imagination was as powerful as that kiss had been, and suddenly her long-held resolve to save herself for marriage seemed like an empty threat, because she knew, without doubt, that if Jake pushed her just a tiny bit that resolve would crumble to dust.

He didn't, though. He didn't push her, either that day, or a week later, when they'd been out for a drink in the evening and he brought her home and they sat in his car outside and he kissed her until her body was screaming.

'I need a coffee,' he said after a few more minutes, when their searing passion had cooled just a little.

'Sure. Come on in.'

It was quiet in the house, all the lights out except the kitchen light that they'd left on for her. 'They've gone to bed,' she told him, and he sighed.

'Did you have to use that word?'

'What? Bed?' she teased.

They put the kettle on, and while it boiled he pulled her into his arms again and rocked her against his chest.

'I need you,' he groaned into her hair. 'I want to make love to you.'

'Uh-uh,' she murmured, moving back out of his arms. 'No. Not until I'm married. I know it's old-fashioned, but I always said I'd be a virgin on my wedding night, and I'm not going to let a sweet-talking charmer like you talk me out of it.'

He caught her hands and drew her closer again, staring down into her eyes with curious intensity.

'I'd better marry you, then, hadn't I?' he said lightly, just as Mel walked in.

'Oh, my God, you're getting married!' she shrieked, and, laughing, she hugged them both and laughed and cried.

'Hey, hang on,' she tried to say, but she was drowned out by the arrival of her parents.

'They're getting married!' Mel told them, and she was swept along in the ensuing hubbub.

And it was only weeks later, when she'd stood in

the marquee and really thought about what she was doing, that she realised she'd never said yes to his proposal, and he'd never, even once, told her that he loved her...

CHAPTER FIVE

'THANK goodness you're back! I was beginning to wonder what on earth had happened to you!'

Lydia gave herself a mental shake and dragged herself back to the present. There was no point in trawling through the past all over again, she told herself, and opened the door, summoning what she hoped was a convincing smile for her mother. 'Sorry. We went strawberry-picking and got carried away.'

'You don't have to tell me—you've got juice all over your hands. Did you get lots?'

'Yup—I'm going to make a summer pudding.'

'Oh, lovely! Oh, did you remember my hat, by the way?'

'Yes, of course. Anyway you know Jake wouldn't have let me forget it.'

'And how was the dress?' Maggie asked, helping to take the brimming punnets of fruits into the kitchen.

'Fine. She can take it in. I have to go back on Wednesday morning.'

'I fed her cake,' Jake told her mother, coming up behind them with the last of the fruit, 'and I've never seen anyone put away strawberries like it, so I hope they aren't too fattening. I doubt if the dress will fit by Wednesday if she keeps on eating like she's done today.'

'Well, she could do with putting a bit on. At least

she's looking more relaxed than when she came back,' Maggie said, studying her daughter assessingly.

'Excuse me, I am here?' Lydia said, dumping the currants on the worktop and glaring at them both.

Her mother laughed and hugged her. 'You're gorgeous. I don't care how fat or thin you are; it's lovely to have you home. I've missed you. We've all missed you.'

Over her mother's shoulder she caught a flicker of what could have been pain on Jake's face, and felt a stab of guilt. She was beginning to think he had cared for her, perhaps more than he'd said, but he was still giving nothing away.

Maybe the party in London would give them a chance to explore their feelings away from her inquisitive and interfering family.

'Right, I need to get on,' he said, heading for the door. 'I've got calls to make.'

'Can't you stay for a cup of tea?' Maggie asked, sounding disappointed, but he shook his head.

'No time. Sorry. Maybe another day.'

Odd, how empty the room felt without him.

Her mother gave her a searching look. 'Are you OK?' she asked gently, and Lydia nodded.

'Yes. I'm OK.' Confused, churned up, but alive, at least, for the first time in a year. 'I'm OK,' she repeated, and picked up the fruit. 'Right. About this summer pudding. I thought I'd make one for us and one for Jake.'

'Or you could make a big one and we could invite him for supper tomorrow. He often eats with us when he's up here. Why don't you suggest it?'

And have to spend the evening in his company with all her family looking on and hanging on their every word? Still, it was better than spending the evening without him, she acknowledged. 'OK. I'll talk to him when I see him.'

'When you see who?' Mel asked, coming into the kitchen with Tom right behind her, his hands on her shoulders.

'Jake. Mum wants to ask him for supper tomorrow.'

'I'll ask him,' Tom offered, sliding his arms around Mel's waist and kissing her neck.

'You two are revolting,' Lydia said in mock disgust, and turned away. She wasn't really disgusted, just jealous, if she was honest. Since she'd been back Jake had kissed her twice, once on her return, once last night, and each time had been just a fleeting touch of his lips.

She ached for more, for the intimacy and familiarity that Mel and Tom shared, but it wasn't about to happen.

'Are you staying for supper, Tom?' Maggie was asking, and Lydia found herself wondering what Jake was doing for supper and if he ought to join them tonight, as well as tomorrow.

'I think Jake's planning on nipping back to town tonight to catch up on some work, and picking up our suits in the morning, so probably not. I thought I'd go with him and sort out a few things at the flat— Mel, are you coming with me?'

'No, she's not,' her mother said firmly. 'There's far too much to do. I'm surprised at you, Tom—and I'm still cross because you whisked her away this morning.'

'It wasn't me!' Tom protested laughingly. 'She dragged me off! She's a wicked woman, your daughter, and you should know that by now.'

Maggie humphed, and Lydia hid a smile. She could well believe it was the flighty Mel and not her reliable and honest and incredibly long-suffering Tom who was behind their escape that morning.

'I think that's your answer,' Mel said with a wry smile, and followed Tom out of the door. Five minutes later she came back with a pretty colour in her cheeks and her lips all rosy and swollen, and there was a glow in her eyes that nothing could disguise.

Lucky girl, Lydia thought again.

'So, it's just us for supper,' Maggie said with a warm smile at her daughters. 'That'll be nice.'

It was nice. It was cosy and friendly and without stress, and Lydia had an early night and finished the book she'd started on the plane, and then she went to sleep and dreamed of Jake's pale cream bedroom and that big high bed and his arms strong around her, and when she woke, her pillow was damp and her face was wet with tears.

She answered the phone the following morning at ten, and it was Jake. 'Hi, we're in town. We're just going to pick up the suits now, but I gather your mother asked me to join you for supper tonight.'

'That's right,' she confirmed, and found herself waiting with bated breath.

'I've got a better idea. Why don't you all come to me? I'll cook.'

'Can you?' she said doubtfully, and he laughed.

'I'm thirty, Lydia,' he reminded her. 'Of course I can cook. How do you think I survive? Takeaways?'

'Probably,' she replied. 'Anyway, I've done the summer pudding.'

'Bring it. It can be the centrepiece, and we can fall back on it when all else fails. I'll expect you around seven—unless you want to come and help me?'

She discovered she did want to. 'What time?' she asked, and she could almost hear him thinking.

'Five? You can do the veg. I hate peeling carrots but I thought I'd do a pork loin and julienne carrots go really well.'

'OK, I'll come at five with my apron on and find out just how wrongly I designed your kitchen.'

He laughed. 'OK. See you later. You can help me test the wine.'

She cradled the phone and sighed, and then turned to find her mother watching her curiously.

'Was that Jake?' she asked, and Lydia nodded.

'Yes. He wants us to go to him for supper.'

'Oh, good, he's a wonderful cook and I'm so busy with the run-down to this wedding I think I'm going to scream. Darling, could you do me a favour before you go over there and put the wedding presents out in the dining room? We don't need to eat in there again before the wedding and there are so many stacked up now. Besides, everyone will want to look at them. They need labels—I've left the cards with each of the presents. It should be fairly obvious.'

It was, of course—obvious and familiar. She'd done the same thing last year, and all for nothing. Well, maybe not nothing. Mel and Tom had packed them all up and returned them, and because of that they'd grown to love each other.

Whereas she and Jake—

She switched her mind off and concentrated on the display, and by the time she'd finished it was lunchtime and the presents looked wonderful.

'All done,' she told her mother, settling down at the kitchen table and helping herself to coffee from the cafetière. "Anything else I can do?'

'Not for a moment. Stay and talk to me. I've just had a call from the breeder we got Molly from, to tell me that Molly's niece has just had a litter of twelve puppies, six of each. I've reserved a bitch and we've got to go and choose her after the wedding. Want to come?'

'I'd love to. It seems really strange here without a dog. I think it's the first time.'

'It is, but with the wedding coming up I didn't think I could concentrate on a new puppy, and anyway, I wanted one of Molly's relatives. She was such a sweetie, and I do miss her.'

They fell silent, each remembering the dear old dog who'd been part of their lives for so long, and then Maggie sighed and stood up. 'I've got a client coming this afternoon—I couldn't put her off, she was quite determined, so I suppose it might be an idea if I was ready for her.'

'Shall I throw something together for lunch?' Lydia offered.

'Bless you. Your father's in the farm office; give him a shout when you're done. Mel's at the florist sorting out a hitch; she shouldn't be long.'

She made a salad, crisp and fresh and cool on this

muggy late June day, and then wandered down to the farm office to tell her father it was ready. As she did so, she saw Jake's car go along the lane, and her heart kicked against her ribs.

Silly, really, that she should feel so much more alive just because he was in range again. She was going to have to get over it, because he was leaving as soon as the house was sold.

She shook her head as if to clear out the unpleasant thoughts, and stuck her head round the office door.

'Hiya, Lydia. Welcome home,' the farm manager said with a smile. 'Come in, you don't have to hover. Can I do anything for you?'

She returned his smile and stepped inside. 'Hello, Jim. I was only looking for my father. I thought he was here.'

'He won't be long. He's just gone up to the top fields with Andrew to check the barley. It's almost ready for combining—can't believe it. The season's so advanced.'

'We picked raspberries and redcurrants yesterday as well as strawberries,' she told him. 'They're very early.'

They chatted for a while about the weather and the state of the farming industry, and Jim's new baby, and how their other two were getting on, but all the time her attention was elsewhere, just a short distance down the road in a house that she loved almost as much as her family home. How could he bear to leave it?

'Hello, darling. Are you looking for me?'

She turned towards the door and smiled at her fa-

ther. 'Yes. Lunch is ready when you are. It's salad.
It'll keep, if you're busy.'

'Never too busy for food,' he said with a chuckle,
and slung his arm round her shoulders. 'Heavens, girl,
you're fading away. Come on let's go and feed you
up a bit. I'll be back in half an hour, Jim. See you
then.'

'OK, boss.'

They went up to the house, and there in the kitchen
were Jake and Tim, propped up against the worktop
and shrinking the kitchen with their rugged bulk.

'Can you stretch the lunch?' Maggie asked, and she
shrugged, trying to quell the enthusiastic beating of
her heart.

'Sure. I'll slash up a bit more salad. There's plenty
of ham and chicken and cheese.'

'I made sure there was,' Maggie said with a laugh.
'The last thing I wanted to think about this week was
food.'

'You'll be lost when it's all over and you've got
nothing to fuss about,' Raymond said, giving her a
hug, and Lydia watched as her mother swatted him
laughingly and pushed him out of the way.

'Wash your hands,' she instructed, getting the last
word as usual, and he smiled indulgently and turned
on the tap. Lydia sighed softly and wondered if she'd
ever find anyone she felt that easy with. Even with
Jake, whom she adored, she felt tense and edgy most
of the time.

All those unresolved issues, probably, and the re-
sult of a guilty conscience.

Mel drove up just as they were sitting down, and
came in and hugged Tom from behind, wrapping her

arms over his shoulders and across his chest and kissing his upturned face. 'How was London?' she asked.

'Busy. Crowded. Still, the flat's tidier than it was and I cleared out the fridge.'

'Amazing. I should think it was growing large purple flowers by now.'

'Just about,' he said with a laugh, and she pulled up a chair next to him and dived into the salad.

'So, what's for supper, Jake?' she asked, reaching for the salad dressing. 'Are we going to be all right, or will we all be down with food poisoning for the wedding?'

'I expect so,' he said drily. 'I'll add a dash of fresh salmonella to the gravy, just to be on the safe side, and the pudding's got raw egg in it.'

'Liar, it's summer pudding,' Lydia corrected, and he grinned.

'One of the puddings, I should have said.'

She groaned. 'You're determined to try and make sure that dress doesn't fit, aren't you?' she complained, and he chuckled.

'What dress?' Mel said, looking alarmed. 'Not the bridesmaid's dress? Don't you dare eat too much!'

Lydia put down her fork with a laugh. 'There's no pleasing you lot,' she grumbled good-naturedly, and looked to Jake for rescue. 'I don't suppose you want help all afternoon, do you?'

He chuckled. 'If you like. There's not that much to do, but I'm sure I can find something. You can dust the attic or something, if you want.'

'Sounds good,' she said drily. 'Anything rather than stay here and get teased and tormented.'

They all laughed at her, but in a way she was serious. All the camaraderie and jollity was beginning to get on her nerves, and she didn't know if she'd get through the week. She just wanted somewhere to go and be quiet, and Jake's lovely kitchen with the bleached oak units and the view of the garden seemed like a good place to start.

Suddenly the fact that they didn't talk very much seemed a positive asset!

'Coffee?' Maggie offered, but Jake shook his head.

'I've got dinner to get, so I won't, thank you. I need to press on.'

Lydia looked up at him as he stood, and he jerked his head towards the door, eyebrows raised in question.

'Good idea,' she murmured, pushing back her chair. 'Mel, Tom, you can clear up, can't you, darlings? I'll go and keep the salmonella under control.'

She followed Jake out, and as she went through the door she could hear Mel sighing softly under her breath. 'We know what you're do-ing' and her mother's quick shushing.

Had Jake heard? Please, God, no, she thought, and for once she thought fate might be on her side. He was getting into his car, the passenger door hanging open for her, and she slid into the seat and closed the door and sighed.

'You can have too much of a good thing, can't you?' he said with a chuckle, and she rolled her head on the seat and smiled at him.

'Thank you for understanding. I was going to go potty.'

'They're good people.'

'I know. It's just, after a year away, it can be a little claustrophobic.'

Claustrophobic? Was that just her family, or family life in general, or people in general, and was he included—or would he be, given time? God only knows, he thought.

He sighed under his breath and started the engine, drove the short distance to his house and lifted out the garment bags from the back of the car.

'You couldn't bring the hats in, could you?' he asked Lydia, and she followed him with the two boxes, in through the gleaming white-painted front door and up the mended stairs to his bedroom.

He hung the garment bags on the outside of his wardrobe and turned to take the hats from her, and surprised a look of longing and sadness on her face.

She was staring at the bed but what she was longing for and sad about he didn't begin to hazard a guess at.

It could have been the room, or him, or the bed itself, or the whole institution of marriage, or an escape from her parents—almost anything, and he was fairly sure he was well down the list.

'Coffee?' he suggested, and she jumped slightly and turned to him with a strained smile.

'Thanks, that would be lovely. What shall I do with these?'

'I'll put them down.'

He dumped them unceremoniously beside the wardrobe and ushered her out of the room where she featured in altogether too many of his dreams. Once safely in the kitchen things should be a little better, he thought.

He put the kettle on, and she settled down on a tall stool at the work island and propped her head on her hands and smiled. 'I do like this kitchen,' she told him in satisfaction.

'Good. So do I.'

'So it all went OK, the installation and everything?'

'Absolutely. They were in and out in no time, and everything worked.'

She laughed. 'That must be a record.'

'I'm sure it isn't. It's been much admired by all the people looking at the house.'

Her face seemed to close up a little. 'Any news on that?' she asked.

'The woman who wanted to steal the dog bed wants it, apparently, and so do the couple who came round on Saturday morning. There's supposed to be someone else coming tomorrow, but I might put them off as we're going to London. If they're keen they'll still be here in a few days.'

And, anyway, since Lydia had said what she'd said about selling something you cared for to total strangers, he suddenly felt ambivalent about passing the house on to someone else.

Besides which, once it was sold he wouldn't see her again, and, masochist that he was, he wasn't sure he was quite ready to take that step yet. He made the coffee in a thoughtful silence, and slid hers across the island to her. 'Cheers,' he said, and, pulling up a stool, he sat down and cradled the mug, inhaling the steam and concentrating on the aroma—anything to blank out the thought of not seeing her again.

'So, what's for supper? Did you get the pork?'

He nodded. 'And carrots and sugar snap peas and baby new potatoes, and cooking apples to make apple sauce, and I thought I'd make a chocolate roulade to go with the summer pudding.'

She looked surprised, and he thought yet again how little they really knew about each other. He wanted to ask her about Leo. He'd been thinking about the man for the last twenty-four hours, but the feeling he was feeling seemed a great deal like jealousy, and it was absurd to be jealous of a dead man.

Except that competing with a ghost was impossible. He'd had an affair with a young widow in the past, and it had all fallen apart because he couldn't walk in the dead man's shadow. He wasn't in a hurry to try and do it again—and anyway, he still hadn't got to the bottom of why she went away.

Maybe the next night would bring some answers.

It was a fun evening. Her family—mercifully!—left her alone, and Mel and Tom were the ones that came in for the ribbing this time, so Lydia was able to relax and enjoy herself.

The food was wonderful. Her mother was right; he was an excellent cook. There was nothing fancy about the meal, just good ingredients cooked to perfection, and simply presented.

It was the best way to eat, she thought, and often hardest to do, because everything had to be perfectly co-ordinated. It shouldn't have surprised her, of course, that an engineer could time things accurately and remain unflustered, but her father couldn't boil water, so it was a sexist thing, she admitted to herself.

Her parents went home at ten, and Lydia volunteered to stay and help clear up.

Tom and Mel looked grateful, and disappeared for a 'walk' in the garden, and they were alone together.

'That was lovely,' she told him honestly, and he gave her a patient smile.

'I told you I could cook.'

'You could just be gracious,' she grumbled, and he laughed and took the heavy stack of plates from her and put them in the dishwasher.

'I could, but I'm not. I know my strengths and weaknesses.'

'What are your weaknesses?' she asked him teasingly, and for a second his smile faltered.

'You,' she thought she heard him say under his breath, but she must have imagined it; it must just have been an exhalation.

'I don't have any I'll admit to,' he said lightly, and disappeared back into the dining room.

She followed him, collecting up the last of the glasses and spare cutlery, and within minutes the place was back to normal.

'I'll walk you home,' he said.

'There's no need; it's only just next door.'

'I know that. I'll still walk you home.'

She knew him well enough to realize that he wouldn't give up, so she wriggled her feet back into her shoes, picked up her bag and smiled.

'OK, I'm ready.'

'I'll leave a note for Mel and Tom. I think they're in the summer house. It's a lovely evening.'

It was a lovely evening. A clear, navy sky shot with gold, tiny bright stars twinkling overhead like diamonds. The scent of honeysuckle was heavy on the air, and the nicotiana and night-scented stocks beside the drive were wonderful. She breathed deeply, and sighed in ecstasy.

'Gorgeous, isn't it?' he murmured, and then she felt his arm round her shoulders, holding her against his side. As they walked she felt the bump of his hip against hers, and she fell naturally into step with him, like a three-legged race without the string, she thought inconsequentially.

It felt good to be so close to him—good and a little unnerving. Was he just playing with her, or was he genuinely trying to rebuild their bridges to make the future easier?

Almost certainly he wasn't doing it for the reasons she would have chosen, she thought, but then as they approached her house he drew her to a halt just out of the circle of light and turned her gently into his arms.

'Thank you for your help today,' he murmured, and before she could say anything, his hand cradled her face and his lips met hers and he was kissing her as she'd wanted him to kiss her for days.

She melted against him, her hands clinging to his shirt, bunching it in fists and hanging on like grim death in case it should all fade away like a dream dissolving with the return of wakefulness.

But it didn't fade, it grew, consuming her, and when he lifted his head she gave a tiny cry of protest and drew him back to her again. He didn't argue, but the next time he raised his head he took her hands and lifted them to his lips.

'Your parents are in the kitchen,' he said softly. 'I

don't want them giving you any grief for this. And anyway, there's always tomorrow.'

Tomorrow, she thought, when she was going to London with him and spending time alone with him, staying in his converted loft that Mel had been raving about, going to the party with him, and then back to his place for the night.

A shiver of anticipation ran through her, and he released her gently. 'I must go. Thanks for your help. I'll see you tomorrow morning at ten, shall I? We can go and get your dress, and then head off.'

'What shall I bring?' she asked, thinking of the party and wondering what on earth she had to wear.

'Nothing fancy,' he said to her relief. 'It's only casual—a barbecue. It should be fun. Your blue dress? Oh, and bring something to swim in; they've got a pool.'

A pool? Her blood pressure nearly went off the scale. She'd never seen him in less than trousers and a shirt—jeans and a T-shirt with bare feet the most casual he'd ever been in the short time she'd known him. And now, maybe, she'd see very, very much more of him.

He bent his head and kissed her again, then murmured, 'Goodnight, Princess,' so softly it was almost lost on the light night breeze. Then he turned on his heel and walked swiftly away, his feet crunching on the gravel, and when she could no longer see or hear him, she turned and went inside, her lips still tingling from his kiss and her heart singing, because tomorrow she was going with him to London and maybe, just maybe, she'd get another chance...

CHAPTER SIX

'GOT everything?'

Lydia nodded, dropped her head back against the head restraint and sighed hugely. 'Yes, I've got everything,' she said, and then had a moment of doubt. She rolled her head towards him. 'Well, not *everything*, exactly, but you didn't imply I'd need much. I've got a dress and a swimsuit and a towel and a change of clothes and wash things—that do?'

His deep, rich chuckle filled the car and sent a shiver through her. 'I expect that'll do fine. Let's hit the road, then, before they find something else to detain you with.'

'I'm sure they'll cope without me,' she said drily, only too glad to get away from the wedding preparations that were like rubbing salt into the wound. She wasn't sure what was worse—watching Mel and Tom and envying them their happiness, or being with Jake and thinking about what might have been.

Common sense dictated that neither of them were really good for her, but for now she was here, right next to him, and she wasn't about to argue.

The car was smooth and quiet and ate up the road with civilised ease, and she was happy to relax and let the miles slip past without talking. Strange, she thought, how they seemed to get on best when they *weren't* talking!

After collecting her dress it didn't seem like long

before they were on the outskirts of London, and then predictably they slowed down, but at last they turned left before the Tower, drove over Tower Bridge and then they were there, and he was ushering her into his apartment.

She'd been right, of course, to assume it was prestigious, but it was more than that. It was a home, his home, filled with his things, personal in a way that so much of the house in Suffolk hadn't yet become and never would, now, if he sold it. It was, in a way, the real Jake Delaney, the man she'd never met, and her curiosity knew no bounds.

Her eyes took in every little detail—the huge sliding doors opening to a glass balcony that overlooked the river, the soaring ceiling, the black iron spiral staircase rising up to the mezzanine level built at one side by the floor-to-ceiling window, with a kitchen area beneath and a door to what were probably the bedrooms—

Or bedroom? Her heart pounded, and she forced herself to concentrate. She could sleep on the floor if necessary—if she wanted to.

White walls, bleached wood floors, black iron beams spanning the vast expanse of roof, everything very clean-cut and modern and yet managing to be homely in a curious way.

A mug had been left on the slab of wood that passed for a coffee table, a casually folded newspaper next to it, and the deep charcoal-grey suite in butter-soft suede looked comfortably broken in and inviting. Yes, it was spectacular, but it also managed to be welcoming, and she felt herself starting to relax.

'Cup of tea?' he offered, and she nodded.

'Please…'

She trailed off, drawn by the wall of glass, and after a moment he appeared beside her and slipped the catch, and the doors slid back out of the way, giving her access to the balcony. She stepped out, breathing in the smell of the river and the bustling city beyond, and was fascinated.

'You can see Tower Bridge from here, on your left.'

She turned her head, and there it was, its distinctive square towers clearly visible in the shimmering air. Beneath her people strolled along the riverbank, and boats chugged slowly through the murky water, leaving a softly foaming wake that vanished almost instantly.

'It's lovely here.'

He laughed softly from behind her. 'You sound surprised.'

'I am surprised. Not that it's wonderful, but that I like it—that it isn't so sharp-edged and ultra that I feel uncomfortable.'

'And are you comfortable?'

'Oh, yes,' she assured him, turning slowly and smiling. 'I'm comfortable. It's extraordinarily peaceful, considering it's central London. I can see why you want to spend more time here, in a way.'

Their eyes met, and something flickered in the back of his, then he turned aside. 'I'll show you your room,' he said, answering one of her questions, and, picking up her case, he headed for the door she'd noticed. 'It doesn't have a balcony, I'm afraid, but it still looks over the river and it's got its own bathroom.'

Like the rest of the apartment, it was very simple. Almost monastic, but it worked—a simple bed with crisp white bedding in a room with white walls and a wooden floor, with a bright modern rug the only concession to colour. A door stood ajar, and she glimpsed a white bathroom tiled from floor to ceiling, the fittings modern and very upmarket.

'I'll leave you to freshen up,' he said. 'I'll make the tea and pour it when you come out.'

He put her little bag on a stand at the foot of the bed, and she thanked him and waited till he'd gone, then crossed to the window. So many people out there being so busy, she thought, and wondered how many of them were happy and how many, like her, had no idea what the future held for them.

She was relieved that he wasn't apparently expecting her to sleep with him, but she was conscious too of a lingering disappointment. She had hoped his invitation meant more than just an excuse to get away, but maybe she'd misread it.

She used the bathroom, with its Villeroy and Boch suite, and thought the taps alone probably cost more than the average family bathroom refit. Clean, pure lines, form and function inextricably linked to make utilitarian items things of beauty. Attention to detail, she thought, and was stunned that he'd chosen their family firm to design his kitchen, and that he'd allowed her such a free rein, because he clearly had a huge amount of money and could have afforded anyone.

No doubt his women fell into the same category— rich, professional and well-groomed without doubt. She gave her hair a despairing look in the mirror, dragged a brush through it and went back out into the living area.

He was nowhere to be seen, so she went into the kitchen and had a good look round.

Slick wasn't the word. It was stainless steel, very high-tech, as he'd said, everything very ultra.

Quite, quite different from his bleached oak farmhouse kitchen in the house, and although she admired its faultless execution, she didn't like it.

She heard a footstep overhead and looked up, just as he ran lightly down the spiral stairs and turned towards her with a smile. 'OK?' he asked, and she nodded.

'Fine. I was just snooping at the kitchen.'

He shrugged. 'I prefer the other one. This is a bit alternative for me—a bit too cutting edge, but it's a very functional kitchen and it's good to work in—talking of which, have you poured the tea?'

She hadn't, of course, because she'd been too busy looking round at everything. She smiled apologetically. 'As it's still in the pot, I don't suppose I could be unbelievably nosy and see the rest of the flat, could I?'

He looked for a moment as if he'd like to say no, but then he shrugged. 'Sure, why not? There isn't much. Your bedroom, another bathroom and my office down here. I sleep over here,' he said, pointing up at the ceiling. 'Come and see. It's not overwhelmingly tidy at the moment, but it has a stunning view.'

She followed him up the stairs through an opening in the low plate glass barrier and onto the mezzanine floor, and her jaw dropped.

The bed was low, a futon probably, with a white

quilt pulled up roughly over the bottom sheet, the pillows abandoned half-on, half-off the floor. It looked as if the last time he'd slept here he'd had a restless night, and she remembered it had been Sunday, after she'd gone over for breakfast and he'd come down to London afterwards to spend some time in the office.

He yanked the quilt straighter and dropped the pillows back on the bed with an apologetic grimace, but her attention had moved on to the window. The floor cut across the glass wall halfway up, and the bed lay so close to it that you could probably see right down to the river without moving.

'Wow,' she said softly, and he gave a low laugh.

'Yes. It is a pretty wonderful place to sleep. The moon can be a bit annoying sometimes, but I couldn't bear to shut it out with curtains.'

'Aren't you worried you'll be seen?'

He laughed. 'What, up here? Who's going to see me, apart from the seagulls? No one—and anyway, I've got nothing to hide. I can lie in bed in the morning and watch the sun come over the horizon, and it's the most wonderful feeling in the world.'

'No wonder you always wake up early,' she said with a laugh, and wished she could wake up with him to the feel of the sun on her face and his arms around her.

She dragged her eyes reluctantly away from that side of the room and looked around the rest of the raised level. There was a door at the far side leading to what she imagined was a bathroom, and several more doors beside it that looked like wardrobes and cupboards.

A thick white wool rug covered the pale polished

boards, but everything was low-key, with nothing to detract from the simplicity of the design or the stunning view of London. She looked down on the sitting area below, where the pair of two-seater sofas sat opposite each other in the centre with the coffee table slab between them, spaced just right to put your feet up and snooze.

'It's beautiful,' she said wistfully.

Beautiful, and she could have been sharing it with him—

'Fancy a walk by the river?' he suggested, and she jumped at it. Anything rather than sit around in here and regret things she couldn't change.

They went down in the lift and out onto the walk outside, strolling along like tourists as he pointed out the sights—the Tower of London, huge and forbidding, the place where so many people had spent their last days before being taken out and hung in times past; *HMS Belfast*, moored opposite the Tower, just a little upriver from Jake's apartment; the galleries, shopping malls and restaurants of the rich and trendy.

No wonder he's coming back here to live full-time, she thought dismally. Suffolk can't hold a candle to this.

And yet, given the choice, she knew where she'd rather live—in the peaceful river valley where she'd been born and raised, on the farm that had been in their family for six generations.

Or next door to the farm, in Jake's beautiful and empty house that was just crying out for children and dogs and cats and all the paraphernalia of family life. Family life they could have brought to it.

Oh, damn.

She blinked back the tears and turned away from him, pretending interest in something on the other side of the river to hide her eyes from him until the prickling stopped and she felt safe again.

They stopped for tea in a pavement café, since they'd neglected the pot he'd made, and after a while he glanced at his watch. 'We ought to be heading back, I suppose; it's nearly five. It'll take us some time to get there in the evening traffic, and it starts at eight. How long will it take you to get ready?'

She shrugged. 'Not long. Half an hour at the most? I'll have a quick shower, but I washed my hair this morning and if I'm swimming there's no point in doing it again.'

His hand came up and lifted a strand, sifting it through his fingers with a strange expression on his face. 'It's lovely hair,' he murmured. 'Soft and glossy—it feels like silk.'

She was frozen to the spot, her breath jammed in her throat, her skin covered in tiny pinpricks in reaction to his nearness. Then abruptly he dropped his hand and stood up. 'We ought to get back anyway. I've got a couple of calls to make.'

Her brow creased in a little frown as she hurried after him. What was wrong with him now? Unless, of course, he still felt the same about her...

This evening might turn out to be quite revealing, she thought with a quiver of anticipation—mingled with fear, because, of course, what was revealed might not be what she wanted to know...

Dear God, she was lovely. She was frolicking in the water with some of the other girls, playing water polo, and he was sitting on the side with his feet in the water watching her with a face that would probably have been a dead giveaway if it hadn't been for the cover of the darkness.

Steam curled off the surface of the heated water and wreathed the bushes in the vicinity in eerie wisps of mist. Coloured lights were strung through the trees, and on the other side of the pool the barbecue was still going strong.

His attention came back to Lydia, and his throat seemed to close. The underwater lights illuminated her legs as she trod water and then dived for the ball, her slender body arching through the air as her hands fastened on it and flipped it through the hoop at the end.

A great cheer went up, and he gave a wry smile. She'd been in there for ages, she'd be like a wrinkled prune soon, but she was happy, and it was wonderful to see.

'Hey, you guys, come on in, we need more bodies!' one of the girls called, and someone grabbed his ankle and he found himself hauled into the water unceremoniously.

He came up laughing and found himself face to face with Lydia.

'Was that you?' he asked, and she smiled innocently.

'Me?' she said. 'Would I?'

'Very likely. Am I on your team?'

'No!' the other girls chorused. 'We want him!'

He smiled slightly and shrugged, and went up to the other end. It had its definite advantages, of course, he was to discover. Playing opposite her meant tackling her, and every now and again he found her slim, willowy body pressed against his as she squirmed to get the ball from him.

And because the rule book seemed to have got lost, he ended up holding her still while the ball flew overhead, trapping her against his body with one strong arm while the other flipped the ball back towards his own team.

'Cheat!' she laughed, and he looked down into her eyes and froze, suddenly desperately aware of her softness against him and the betrayal of his body.

He released her and moved away, but not before she'd felt the telltale stirrings of his desire. Their eyes were still locked, hers wide and soft, and then he dragged his own away and turned his attention back to the game with furious intensity.

Finally it was over, and he hauled himself up onto the side with one easy thrust of his arms and wrapped the towel firmly round his waist. She was standing a few feet away, her nipples pebbled in the cool night air, and desire tore through him again and shredded his control.

'Can we go?' he asked, and after a startled second she nodded her head.

'Yes, of course. I'll just get dressed.'

She disappeared, and he found his clothes in a bedroom and pulled them on over a body that was still wet, such was his haste.

'You can't go!' their host said a few minutes later as they made their goodbyes.

'Sorry, we've got an early start in the morning,'

he lied, and then they were walking down the pavement towards his car, an uneasy silence between them.

They reached the car without a word being exchanged, and as he slid behind the wheel she turned to him.

'Did I miss something?' she said, and he let out his breath on a ragged sigh.

'I'm sorry. It's just—watching you like that—you don't make it easy. You're a beautiful woman, Lydia. I can't just switch off my feelings simply because it's all over between us.'

'Is it?' she said softly.

He stopped dead. 'Is what?' he asked, hardly able to believe his ears.

'Is it all over? The way you kissed me last night— I rather thought it might not be.'

He stabbed trembling fingers through his wet hair. His chest was heaving, his heart was pounding and he felt almost sick with anticipation.

'What are you saying, Lydia?' he asked, and his voice sounded strangled.

She looked up at him, her face strangely colourless in the streetlight, her eyes unreadable. 'Just that, really—that maybe it isn't over. Maybe there's still something there. Maybe we owe it to ourselves to find out before it's too late.'

He dragged in a lungful of air. He was taking her back to his apartment, where there were no chaperons, no defences, nothing to help him behave like a gentleman except his own guilty conscience—and the way that was behaving lately, it probably wouldn't kick in until morning.

God help me, he thought silently, closing his eyes in despair. I'm not strong enough to do this—

'Jake? I'm sorry. I—I didn't mean to presume. If it's over, just say so. I just thought we had unfinished business, but I could be wrong. I didn't mean to embarrass you.'

'You're not embarrassing me,' he said in the same tortured voice. No, I'm doing that all on my own, he added silently to himself. 'We need to go back to my place and talk about this.'

He turned the key in the ignition, gunned the engine and shot off down the quiet street, then remembered his recent speeding fine and the points on his licence and slowed down. He couldn't afford to gain any more points; he'd still got some from last year when she'd walked out on him and he'd burned up some rubber until the police had caught him and thrown the book at him, and absolutely the last thing he needed was to lose his licence altogether.

Perhaps he'd buy a little electric car so he couldn't speed, he thought with wry disgust, and concentrated on obeying the letter of the law all the way home.

It was a good idea, anyway. It took his mind off Lydia, and that had to be an improvement...

He was grimly silent all the way back to his apartment, and Lydia's heart was pounding by the time they got there. Was he angry with her? With himself? With both of them?

Did he love her, or just want her? Because he did want her; she knew that without doubt.

A bit of her, long denied, didn't care why he wanted her, just that he did. Never mind her long-held beliefs. They'd caused nothing but trouble last time. Perhaps it was time to dispense with such silly and outdated notions—besides which, this might be the only chance she had, and she didn't want to regret turning it down for the rest of her life.

If she only had this one night with him, then so be it, but she was going to take everything he offered.

They went up to the apartment and he flicked a switch. Soft light spilled from the uplighters and brushed the ceiling with gold, but it didn't detract from the sparkle of the London night outside the wall of windows.

'It's warm,' Jake muttered, and striding over to the doors he slid them open, standing out on the balcony with his hands locked on the rail as if he contemplated throwing himself over.

Her heart in her mouth, she went out and stood beside him, shivering slightly in the cool breeze.

'You're cold,' he said almost accusingly.

'I was in the water a long time.'

'Go and have a hot bath. I'll make you a drink when I've had a shower.'

'Are you OK?' she asked, and he gave her an odd look.

'Of course I am. Why?'

She shook her head and turned away, going back inside into the warmth. Hot bath, he'd said. It sounded like a good idea.

She went into her room, soaked for a while in the blissfully hot water and then rubbed herself briskly dry on towels like thistledown. There was a hairdryer in the vanity unit, and she dried her hair roughly and fingercombed it back from her face, then pulled the dress on again without bothering with underwear.

If she had her way, she wouldn't need it anyway.

He was in the kitchen when she came out, frothing milk with steam from the coffee-maker, and he poured it onto two mugs, sprinkled chocolate powder generously over the top and handed one to her.

'Cappuccino,' he said economically. 'Be careful, it's hot.'

'Thanks.' She took it, sipping at the chocolate-dusted froth to stop it spilling over, then headed for the balcony, her bare feet soundless on the polished boards.

He was wearing jeans again, she'd noticed, but he'd changed into a soft rugby shirt that hung to the top of his thighs. How sensible of him, she thought. She was still cool, even after her hot bath, and she began to wish she'd put on something a little warmer.

The wind changed direction, flirting with the hem of her dress, blowing it against her so that the soft, filmy fabric clung lovingly to her every curve. She shivered slightly, and he moved up behind her, sheltering her from the wind with his big, warm body.

'You're still cold,' he said gruffly.

'Not really cold. It's just the breeze that's a bit chilly.'

He wrapped his arms around her waist, one above the other, so one arm lay against her ribs just below her breasts, pulling the fabric tight over her puckering nipples.

She heard the slight hiss of his indrawn breath, and turned her head a fraction so she could see his face. It was drawn tight, his expression unguarded for once and raw with need, and her heart slammed in her throat.

'So beautiful,' he said roughly, his voice scarcely more than a whisper. His lips brushed the side of her neck, teasing her skin, leaving a trail of fire over her collarbone and down to the hollow of her throat.

His breath burned her cool skin, making shivers run over her like fingers of ice. She laid a hand over his arms, her fingers splayed, her head falling back against his shoulder as he kissed her throat, her neck, her jaw.

Finally he drew her inside, removing the forgotten coffee from her nerveless fingers and setting it down, then he took her back into his arms. Away from the breeze, the heat radiated from his body and engulfed her in flames, and with a shaken sigh she moved closer and lowered her head to his chest. For a while they didn't move, just stood holding each other, swaying gently to the soft music in the background.

She became aware of the words, muted love songs that spoke of heartache and pain, and after an endless moment he lifted his head and looked down at her.

His eyes were burning with a brilliant blue flame, and her knees nearly gave way with the wave of need that ripped through her.

'We need to talk,' he began, but she laid her hand lightly over his lips and shook her head.

'No. We seem to fight whenever we talk, so don't talk. Just make love to me,' she said softly, and for a moment she thought he was going to refuse.

Then his arms tightened slightly and he dropped his head on her shoulder. 'Lydia—'

'Please?'

Slowly, infinitely slowly, he lifted his head and stared down at her, searching her eyes. Then finally he smiled, just the merest quirk of his lips. 'It'll be my pleasure,' he murmured.

Releasing her, he took her hand in his and led her up the spiral staircase to his bed. Flicking aside the quilt, he knelt down in the middle of the futon and drew her down so she knelt in front of him, then he cupped her face in his hands, lowered his head and kissed her.

There was no haste, no apparent urgency, just a thorough, systematic arousal of every nerve-ending in her body. He didn't touch her anywhere else—he didn't need to. She'd been waiting too long for him, over a year, and the first brush of his lips had been enough.

He lifted his head and stared down at her, his chest rising and falling unsteadily. 'Take off your dress,' he said, his voice low and rough with need. 'Let me see you.'

She felt no hesitation or embarrassment. This was Jake, and she loved him as she had never loved any other man. She crossed her arms over her front and grasped the hem, then, straightening, she peeled it over her head and dropped it beside them on the bed.

'Dear God,' he whispered unsteadily. His eyes scanned her naked body, lingering on every curve, every hollow, every plane, then he raised them to her face and she thought the longing in them would unravel her.

'Your turn,' she said in a voice she hardly recognised, and with a muttered oath he stripped off the impeding clothes and drew her down into his arms.

She went eagerly, her mouth finding his lips, his jaw, the hollow of his throat, her hands greedily learning his body, the feel of warm, soft skin like silk over the iron of muscle beneath as he tensed his shoulder and raised himself up to look down at her.

'Princess, wait,' he murmured, catching her exploring hand. 'Stop a moment. Do I need to use anything?'

For a second she stared blankly at him, then his meaning registered and she felt soft colour flood her cheeks. Good grief, how could she have been so stupid? And how could he possibly have thought of anything so—so *irrelevant* at a time like this?

'Please,' she replied, and he rolled away from her, opening the top drawer of the low bedside cupboard.

Moments later he was back beside her, and she felt a tremor of emotion run through her. She was ready for this—more than ready, but now the moment was here she had an instant of regret. This should have been a celebration, their wedding night—and now it was just a Wednesday night in June, nothing remarkable at all.

Then his hand touched her cheek, turning her face towards him as he looked down into it with infinite tenderness.

'Are you sure?' he asked gently.

And then she was, more sure than she'd been of anything in her entire life.

'Yes, I'm sure,' she whispered, and he moved over her, his body trembling under her hands, and they were one...

CHAPTER SEVEN

SHE was asleep, her lashes dark against her cheeks, her mouth soft and rosy, swollen from their kisses, slightly parted. She wasn't a tidy sleeper, he'd discovered. She liked to stretch and sprawl, and she'd spent most of the night draped over him, arms spread wide, head pillowed on his shoulder.

Every now and then she'd make a small sound of contentment and snuggle even closer, and he'd drift into wakefulness and stroke her hair until she settled again.

Now she was lying on her back, legs and arms flung wide, the quilt sliding off her body to reveal her small, perfect breasts. He wedged a pillow behind his shoulders and lay there watching her, as the sun lightened the horizon and a finger of gold crept over the rim of the city.

He felt drained this morning. Drained and confused and somehow saddened. She'd always said she would be a virgin on her wedding night, and yet somewhere along the line between last year and now, that principle seemed to have been abandoned or forgotten.

Leo rose from the dead to taunt him again, and his fists bunched on the quilt, just thinking of another man touching her as he'd touched her last night. Had she responded to Leo as she'd responded to him, with such open joy and delight, such greedy enthusiasm and gentle eagerness?

119

Bile rose in his throat and he eased his leg out from under hers and stood up, looking down on her as she lay unmoving and beautiful in his bed.

At least, he thought, now I'll have something real to dream about.

He pulled on his shorts and vest top and crept down the stairs, socks and running shoes in hand. He used the other bathroom so as not to disturb her, and let himself out, putting his shoes on outside the front door because they squeaked on the wooden boards. He did his stretches, earning a strange look from one of his neighbours who was clearly just coming in after a heavy night out, and then went down in the lift and out onto the pavement.

It was a wonderful morning, cool and fresh and crisp, the best part of what promised to be a hot and muggy day. He set off along the riverbank, following his usual route over Tower Bridge and past the Custom House, over London Bridge and back home via the patisserie.

He picked up *pain au chocolat*, croissants and a small wholemeal loaf, called into an all-night chemist just to be on the safe side, and then walked back to the apartment to cool his muscles down.

He left his shoes by the front door and padded softly over to the kitchen. It might be hours before she woke, and he didn't want to disturb her. Normally he could cope with the morning-after thing, but this time there were so many other issues involved.

He'd made love to an ex in the past, but she'd been older and wiser and it had been a trip down memory lane, not a first night that had come totally out of the blue when all hope for the relationship had been abandoned.

And now, this morning, he didn't know how to act with her. He had no idea of her expectations. Was she just toying with him, dealing with unfinished business, as she'd put it? Or did she truly love him?

God knows, he thought, pouring water into the coffee maker and switching it on. When it was done he took a folding chair and his coffee out onto the balcony and sat there, watching the sun gild the tops of the buildings and bring warmth to the day.

He needed a daisy, he thought morosely. She loves me, she loves me not. Which? Two hot, strong black mugfuls later he was no nearer an answer, and his muscles were screaming from sitting in the cool breeze after his run.

He did his stretches, went upstairs and stood for several minutes just looking at her. She moved, turning over and sliding the rest of the quilt onto the floor, and her smooth golden body stretched slightly and relaxed with a sigh.

Desire rocketed through him, and with a stifled groan he turned and went into the bathroom, closing the door with a soft click.

He needed a shower, blisteringly hot and on full power. He'd tried freezing her out of his system and it didn't work. Maybe he'd burn her out instead.

She woke to the feel of sun on her face and cool air over her back. Her eyes opened, and there in front of her was the Thames, with boats puttering silently up and down like water beetles far below her.

She seemed to have lost the quilt. Lifting her head

and shoulders, she looked around her for Jake, but he wasn't there. She felt a pang of disappointment, but then she realised she could hear water running in the bathroom.

It sounded as if he was having a shower, so she stood up and stretched, wincing at the unfamiliar aches in her body, and went over to the bathroom door.

She tapped on it, but he obviously couldn't hear her, so she tried the knob. It turned, yielding under her hand, and she slipped inside and smiled.

He was in the huge shower cubicle, and the water was hammering down, steaming the room up and fogging all the mirrors.

She gave the shower door an experimental tug, and it swung open, bringing a blast of steam and spray in her direction.

Jake turned, his face unreadable, but his body said all she needed to know. She stepped inside, took the soap out of his hand and proceeded to wash him.

'I've washed,' he told her in a strangled voice.

'Mmm. But *I* haven't washed you.' Her hands explored him thoroughly, and within moments he was trembling under her fingers. He took the soap from her and turned her round, reaching round her to wash her, his big hands soaping her thoroughly and being totally inquisitive and absolutely meticulous while his body brushed against her from behind and made her squirm and wriggle back against him.

Every touch of his hands drove her wild, and she started to shake, needing more. Needing him.

She wasn't alone. He rinsed her, cut the water,

wrapped her in huge fluffy towels and carried her back to bed.

'I'm starving,' she confessed lazily.

'Me, too. Can you be bothered to move?'

'What are the options?'

'We could get dressed and eat on the balcony, or I could bring us breakfast in bed, but that won't get me into the office this morning.'

She considered her sore and aching body, unused to lovemaking and tender now in places she hadn't known she had places, and smiled regretfully. 'Balcony?' she suggested, and for a tiny moment she thought she saw disappointment in his eyes.

Then he stood up, pulled on clean shirt and trousers from his wardrobe while she lay back and admired the definition of muscle on his gorgeous body, and headed down the stairs. 'Five minutes,' he warned her. 'If you're too slow, I might eat all the *pain au chocolat*.'

'*Pain au chocolat?*' she squeaked, and bounced up off the bed, tugged the dress over her naked body and ran down the stairs after him. 'You didn't tell me you'd got *pain au chocolat*!'

'You didn't ask. I bought them at the patisserie this morning.'

'You really are an early bird, aren't you?' she said, smiling happily and utterly content with the way her day had started. She leant against him and reached up for a kiss, and his hands slid round and cupped her bottom.

'Are you going to bother with underwear today?' he asked drily, and she gave him an impish smile.

'I don't know. I might not.'

'Hussy,' he murmured, and gave her a long, lingering kiss. 'Go on, put something else on before we end up back in bed. I have to go into the office this morning and you're distracting the life out of me.'

He was right, of course. She showered again quickly, dressed in jeans and a T-shirt and was back into the kitchen in five minutes dead.

'That was quick.'

'Mmm. I had a shower, too. Unfortunately I didn't stop to get dried, and my jeans were hell to get on. That smell is wonderful.'

He laughed at her and shook his head. 'Go and put the other chair and the table out on the balcony, and I'll put this lot on a tray.'

She set the little table up and wondered, out of the blue, how many other women he'd shared breakfast with on this balcony.

None, apparently, in the last year, but that might be just hearsay. Maybe he just hadn't had an affair, a long-term relationship with anyone this year. That didn't mean he hadn't slept with anyone.

And even with her total lack of experience, she knew that the morning after nearly always involved breakfast.

Didn't it?

So how many? One? A dozen?

Oh, Lord. One was too many. She thought of him touching another woman as he'd touched her, and she felt sick. No, please, she thought desperately. At least, not since he met me. Not if he loves me.

And that, of course, was the six-million-dollar question still. Did he love her? Sure, he'd made love to her with great care and tenderness, but maybe he was just that sort of person. Maybe he was like that with all the dozens of women he made love to.

Oh, no. Please, God, no, not dozens.

'Stop torturing yourself,' she muttered, and jumped as he appeared behind her with the laden tray.

'Stop what?'

'Nothing. I just stubbed my toe,' she lied. 'It's fine.'

'Sure?'

Now he was going to make her feel guilty. 'Yes, I'm sure.'

He settled into one of the chairs, poured the coffee and helped himself to one of the little hot chocolate croissants. 'Dig in,' he said, biting cleanly into it.

Lydia, being Lydia, tore hers up, pulled out the little strips of chocolate and dipped them in the coffee, making him grimace.

'You have some disgusting habits,' he said fondly, and she grinned and dipped the last bit in, sucking it with relish.

'Yum. It almost makes up for not having all that lovely tropical fruit for breakfast. Leo and I used to go the market in Bali and buy all sorts of things—mangoes, rambutans, bananas, papayas—wonderful things that just don't taste the same by the time they've been shipped all round the world in some container that's chilling the drawers off them.'

She licked her fingers and glanced up at Jake. His brows were drawn together and he was glowering down at the river below. 'Jake? Are you OK?' she asked, leaning forwards slightly.

'Yes, I'm fine,' he said with a touch of irritation. 'Just indigestion. I've had too much coffee.'

He reached for another croissant, to her puzzlement, and bit into it almost fiercely.

Funny old indigestion, she thought, but he was obviously preoccupied so she picked up another sticky chocolate confection, curled her feet under her and systematically shredded and ate it, drowning herself in flaky little crumbs.

'I don't suppose you've got a napkin?' she said, looking down at her front, and he glanced at her and rolled his eyes.

'You could always use a plate,' he said mildly. 'Don't worry about the crumbs; the birds'll get them. More coffee?'

'Mmm, please.'

He passed it to her and their fingers brushed and he smiled at her. 'OK?' he said gently, and she realised that whatever had been irritating him had been forgotten or pushed aside.

'OK,' she said with a smile of relief, and the tension seemed to dissipate on the light breeze.

They finished their breakfast, and while they were clearing up he asked her what she wanted to do that morning.

'I have to go to the office for a couple of hours. You're more than welcome but I think you might find it very boring. You could stay here and sleep some more, or read a magazine or something, or you could go shopping and meet me back here or at the office— it's up to you.'

She chewed her lip thoughtfully. 'How about if I potter around here for a little while and then make

my way to the office? I could do with a little cul-
ture—perhaps a gallery or two, the odd exhibition?'

'OK,' he said, nodding slowly. 'I'll give you the
address. Have you got enough money for a taxi, or
would you like me to leave you some cash?'

She shook her head. 'I'm OK. I'll see you there
at—what, twelve?'

'Sounds good. What about your luggage?'

'Luggage?' She laughed. 'You mean that tiny bag
with my dress, toothbrush and wet swimsuit in? I
think I can manage it.'

'If you're sure.'

'I'm sure. I backpacked round the Far East and
Australia, remember?'

His mouth tightened slightly, and she instantly regretted her words. Of course he hadn't forgotten! He
wasn't likely to, was he, considering the manner of
her leaving? Oh, damn.

He slipped his arms into a jacket, shrugged it onto
his shoulders, handed her a card out of his wallet and
kissed her goodbye. 'I'll see you later. Have fun.'

The door closed behind him, and she put the card
in her bag and sat down with a plop on one of the
sofas. Have fun? Maybe, but not likely, not without
him. Time to think, perhaps, to reflect on what had
happened in the last twenty-four hours and where on
earth they went from here, but fun?

She dropped her head back against the cushion and
sighed. She had woken up in such a positive mood,
but somewhere along the line doubts had crept in.

He regretted it. She was almost sure he regretted
it, but of course he was much too much of a gentleman to come out and say so. What was he going to

do? Let the wedding come and go, and then just sell the house and leave Suffolk for good and kiss her goodbye?

The thought was unbearably painful.

Anyway, he'd been eager enough for her this morning, when he'd taken her back to bed after their shower. No sign then of regret, she thought, so maybe she was just imagining it.

She threw her things into her little bag, slung it over her shoulder and set off to explore the area. She had a wonderful time—or she would have done if her discovery of his territory hadn't been marred by the knowledge that she was unlikely to share it with him.

Still, the regeneration of the whole area was interesting, and must have involved massive investment. She had time to dive into a little exhibition, and then was frustrated because there was a picture in it that she really, really wanted to buy for Melanie and Tom for a wedding present, and she didn't have enough money in her account to buy it.

She asked them for a card and slipped it into her bag, meaning to phone them later and arrange to pay for it once she'd persuaded her mother to advance her wages. Then she realised she'd run out of time, and she hailed a taxi and gave the driver the address of the office complex.

'There's a major hold-up near there,' he told her. 'I can take you most of the way, but after that you'd do better to walk.'

She didn't have time to walk, so she ran instead, getting lost once and arriving at the office hot and breathless at ten past twelve. She went through the revolving door into luxury, and her heart sank.

Marvellous, just when she was at her worst, some immaculately dressed young woman with a supercilious attitude was going to give her grief—

'Miss Benton?'

She looked towards the voice and found a middle-aged woman smiling indulgently.

'Yes—sorry, I'm late. The traffic—' she gasped, but the woman waved away her explanation.

'I know, we heard there was a jam. Some lorry's got stuck or something. Goodness, you look awfully hot—did you run?'

She nodded, still getting her breath back, and the woman tutted and came out from behind the desk and ushered her towards a door.

'There's a ladies' through here—go and freshen up and I'll tell him you've arrived. Take as long as you like.'

She went into the marble-tiled room and laid her burning cheeks against the cool wall. Bliss. Why on earth had she worn jeans and a thick T-shirt? It was much too hot today, especially if she was going to run around like that!

She looked longingly at the bag containing her cool, floaty dress. It was screwed up in a ball next to her wet swimming things, and there was no way she could wear it.

Oh, well. She splashed her face and hands in cold water and went back out to find Jake leaning against the reception desk and laughing with the kindly receptionist. Laughing about her? Very likely. He caught sight of her and straightened, coming over to her and brushing her cheeks with his cool fingers.

'You should have taken your time,' he murmured.

'Come up to my office and cool off for a minute—the air conditioning will soon sort you out.'

'Changing into something cooler would sort me out,' she said with a wry laugh. 'Except that my dress is cobbled up in the bottom of my bag—'

'Not a problem,' he said. 'Give it to me.'

'What?'

He held out his hand. 'Give it to me. I'll get it dealt with.'

Bemused, she dropped the bag to the floor, opened it and pulled out the crumpled rag. 'Who on earth are you going to get to deal with that?' she asked in amazement.

'The dry cleaners over the road. Beryl, could you be a love and get someone to run this over the way for Lydia? Thanks.'

He handed the garment to his receptionist, who took it totally in her stride. Lydia thought of the last time she'd had it on, when she'd chased Jake down the stairs in just the dress and a sassy smile, and she had to bite the inside of her cheeks to stop from laughing.

'We'll be in my office,' he was saying. 'If you could have someone bring it up as soon as it's ready, that would be great.'

He led her over to the lift, punched a button to close the door and whisk them up to the top floor, and then turned to her, his mouth twitching.

'Come on, then, let's have it. Why are you laughing?'

She shrugged, suddenly aware of being alone in the lift with him. 'I was just thinking of the last time I wore it,' she said, and his eyes tracked over her, the pupils flaring.

'You looked beautiful in it last night,' he said softly, and she felt heated all over again.

The lift sighed to a halt, the doors gliding open silently, and he ushered her along the corridor.

'Hold my calls, Jerry, please,' he said to his secretary, and Lydia was aware of interested eyes following her progress.

The door swished shut behind them and he turned and drew her into his arms, kissing her hungrily. 'I've been wanting to do that all morning,' he mumbled against her hair. His hands smoothed over her spine, sending shivers down it, and she rested her head against him and sighed.

'I don't want to go back to Suffolk yet,' she said, the words coming out of the blue and surprising her. 'It's been so lovely down here with you, and I don't want it to end yet. The moment we get back there they'll be all over us like fleas on a dog, and I just don't feel ready for it. The marquee will be up and Mel will be bubbling and bouncing, and I don't want to spoil her wedding but it's just all a bit close to home—'

He tipped up her face and silenced her with a gentle kiss. 'If you want to stay longer, we can do that. We can have lunch somewhere and then go back to my place and just relax.'

She searched his face for the regret she thought he'd felt earlier, and found no trace of it. 'Could we? Could we really?'

'Sure. Where do you want to eat?'

She laughed. 'Anywhere I can go in that poor dress. Are they going to press it?'

'I imagine they'll dry clean it, but I don't know. It shouldn't be long; they're very good. Fancy a coffee while we wait, or chilled water or juice, or something stronger?'

'Water—cold water would be lovely.'

There was a dispenser in the corner of his office, she noticed now he'd released her. The corner of his *vast* office. She looked out of the window at yet another stunning view, and shook her head. Heavens. He was much more important than she'd realised.

Insecurity wasn't one of her usual weaknesses, but it attacked her now. What on earth did he see in her? Maybe nothing. Maybe that was why he'd walked away last year, because she'd given him a golden opportunity to escape without having to do the decent thing.

He hadn't seemed to want to escape from her last night, though, or this morning—or was that just a natural male response to an available female?

Oh, good grief, she didn't know enough about it to tell, and she couldn't think straight. She still felt hot and bothered and unbelievably scruffy.

'Fancy a shower?' he suggested. 'If you're still really hot, there's one through that door. Often I don't have time to get home between meetings and I can't bear it if I need a shower and can't have one,' he explained, probably reading her dumbstruck expression.

'Um—that would be lovely.'

'I'd join you,' he said with a regretful smile, 'but I'm expecting a call. I'd better tell Jerry to put it through if it comes. You go ahead—there's a robe on the back of the door; put that on until your dress arrives.'

She wasn't going to argue. She was hot and sticky and the idea of cool water pouring all over her was too wonderful to pass up. She indulged herself until she thought he'd wonder if she'd drowned, then she turned off the tap and reached for the towel, scrubbed herself dry and pulled on the robe.

It smelt of him. His aftershave, to be exact, but it was almost synonymous. She snuggled into it, cool now, and opened the door, to find his secretary in there with her dress.

'Perfect timing,' he said with a smile, and handed Lydia the dress. 'Sling it on, we'll go and get lunch.'

'Did your call come?'

'Yes—I'm free to go until Monday. You can hold the fort, can't you, Jerry?'

'I expect I'll manage,' she said drily, and swished out on four-inch heels.

Lydia couldn't walk in four-inch heels, and had to resist the urge to hate the woman for it. She changed back into her freshly cleaned dress and sandals, put the rest of her things back into her bag and went back out into his office.

'Better?' she asked, and he smiled slowly.

'Lovely. Let's go before I change my mind.'

Lunch was a relaxed affair on board a floating restaurant. They had a sun-dried tomato salad between them as a starter, then pan-fried chicken livers with crusty French bread and a watercress garnish, and finished with a sorbet that defied description.

'That was wonderful,' she said with a laugh, grateful that there was plenty of room in the dress. A hideous thought occurred, on the subject of dresses. 'I hope I haven't put on too much weight by Saturday,' she added, grimacing and patting her stomach. 'Mel will kill me if I can't get into the bridesmaid's dress now it's been altered.'

He shook his head. 'You'll be fine. All this running in the heat of the day will keep it off you, anyway.' He leant back casually in the chair and smiled at her. 'So, tell me, what did you do this morning?'

She ran through what she'd done, and then suddenly remembered the picture. 'I found this little gallery,' she told him. 'There was a wonderful picture—so atmospheric. Boats on a beach in the early morning, all suggestion and practically nothing else. I wanted to get it for Mel and Tom, because it reminded me of when we used to go sailing when we were kids.' She pulled a face. 'I bet it'll go. The exhibition only opened last night, apparently.'

'So why didn't you?'

'No money,' she told him frankly. 'I'm going to ask my mother if I can have an advance on my wages, but since I haven't done anything yet, it seems a bit cheeky.'

'I'll buy it, then. You can owe me.'

She looked at him in astonishment. 'You? Why would you want to do that?'

He gave a short, disbelieving laugh. 'Why is it so hard to imagine I'd lend you the money to buy a picture for my best friend and your sister? It's not as if I can't afford it, Lydia.'

She sighed. 'No, I know. It's just—I wanted to do it myself.'

'So do it. Pay me back. I'm not making an indecent suggestion here, you know,' he pointed out gently.

'I know,' she said with a little laugh. 'I was just surprised. I hadn't even thought of asking you.'

'You should have done,' he scolded. 'Where is it? We can pick it up.'

'But it's in the exhibition—'

'Where?'

Shrugging, she dug in her purse and came up with the card. 'Here—that's it.'

'Oh, Lucy. She'll be all right. I've had lots of stuff from her. I'll ring her—any idea what number the picture was?'

She hadn't got a clue, but she knew what it looked like and where it was, and after a few seconds of conversation with Lucy she was told there was now a red sticker on it. 'I'll hold it for you till you come in,' she promised, and Lydia handed the phone back to Jake gratefully.

'She's holding it for me.'

'Excellent. Shall we go and get it?'

The traffic was now flowing freely again, and it took only a few minutes to get back to the gallery. 'Go in and check it's the right one, and then wait in the car while I sort it out,' he said, hovering by the kerb with the engine running.

Two minutes later they were under way again, the picture safely installed in the back of the car.

'I don't know how you did that. I don't think I want to know,' she said, rolling her eyes, and he laughed.

'Lucy's a friend of my cousin Anthony. I've known her for years—and no, we haven't.'

Colour invaded her face again, and she mumbled something indistinct and waited for the ground to open up. Was she really so transparent?

They left the picture locked in the car when they went up to the apartment, and he opened the doors, put the kettle on and dropped onto the sofa, patting the seat beside him.

'Come and sit down and relax,' he instructed, and she sat, her feet up on the wood-slab table, and sighed a huge sigh of contentment.

'Can we stay here for ever?' she asked sleepily, snuggling down against him, but he didn't reply. Instead he kissed her, and her arms slid round him and welcomed him...

CHAPTER EIGHT

'THE marquee's up.'

Her voice sounded dead and flat to her ears, and she was shocked at how choked she felt. She had really, really thought she'd be able to cope with it, but she discovered she couldn't. Somehow the marquee brought it all home to her, and she found her heart was pounding and her palms were damp.

'I'll come in with you,' he said, but she was so distracted she barely noticed the protective tone to his voice. She was just glad he was there—especially when her mother came running up the garden, clipboard in hand.

'Lydia! Jake! Heavens, we wondered what on earth had happened to you! I thought you were going to a party last night and coming home this morning—'

'Sorry, my fault. I had to go into the office. It took longer that I'd expected, so Lydia had to hang around and wait,' he lied smoothly, covering for her to her eternal gratitude. 'Still, it wasn't all wasted time; she found a present for Mel and Tom.'

'Oh, how lovely, darling. Well done. Look, I'm in the marquee with the flower lady helping with the arrangements, and Mel and Tom are in the study doing some last-minute changes to the seating plan. I have no idea where your father is, but somebody needs to sort out the key for the church. Julie was supposed to get in there this afternoon to do the church flowers, but it's nearly five and we haven't found a key yet so we've had to make a start on the marquee. We've tried to track the vicar down but he's out, and the verger's supposed to have a key but he's visiting his wife in hospital, and the day's disappearing fast—'

'Don't worry, we'll sort it out,' Jake assured her confidently. 'Leave it to us.'

He steered Lydia back towards the car, shut her in and slid behind the wheel before her mother had time to think of anything else for her to do. Seconds later they were on the lane again and she gave a guilty sigh.

'She's panicking. I knew she would be. I should have been here.'

'No, you shouldn't. She'll be fine. She's a highly organised woman and she's doing a grand job. We'll just sort out this key. Any ideas?'

'The cleaner?'

'Who is—?'

She shrugged. 'It used to be Mrs Field, but I don't know if it still is. She'll know, anyway. Let's go and ask her. She lives in Mill Lane.'

Mrs Field was indeed still doing the job, and was most reluctant to yield up her key. 'What if I need to get in and the key isn't there? We don't want the church dirty for the wedding!'

'I'm sure it won't be,' Jake soothed, 'and we'll make sure you get it back in time. When do you need it?'

'Tomorrow afternoon,' she said doubtfully. 'I don't suppose you'll be finished.'

'Yes, we will,' Lydia assured her. 'Absolutely. You'll have your key back by lunchtime, I promise.'

'Don't worry,' Jake soothed, and eased the key from her fingers. 'It'll be all right. I'll make sure it is.'

That seemed to do the trick. She beamed at him and released her hold on the key, and he slipped it into his pocket before she could change her mind and they drove back to the house.

'Well?' Maggie said, coming out of the kitchen looking harassed, with Julie in tow.

He pulled the key out of his pocket and handed it to her, and she hugged him.

'Bless you. I knew you could sort it out.'

'It was Lydia who knew who to ask,' he pointed out fairly, and her mother turned to her and looked at her properly for the first time. She felt colour inching up her throat, and wondered if all the things that had happened to her in the past twenty-four hours were written all over her face.

Apparently not—or at least not so clearly that her flustered mother could see them. 'Thank you, darling,' she said, giving Lydia a quick hug, and then she turned to Julie. 'Right, we'd better go up to the church and start on the flowers. I don't suppose you two would like to help with bringing all the flowers into the church so Julie can arrange them, would you?'

'Sure,' Jake agreed, and Lydia's heart sank.

The last thing she needed was to spend time in the cool, quiet village church where she and Jake should have made their vows—and especially after last night, the night that hadn't been their wedding night.

She didn't regret making love with him, but there was a deep sadness, a recognition that it had almost certainly been their swansong. That was why she hadn't wanted to come back, because there, in the oasis of peace and tranquillity far from all the wedding preparations, they had been able to pretend, and now it was all over and the wheels of fate would start grinding again.

His house would be sold, and he would leave, and she'd be there—

'Hey, it may never happen,' Jake said gently, and she struggled for a smile.

'Sorry. I'm not very good company.'

'You're wonderful company. I don't think I could cope with anyone vibrant and jolly at the moment,' he murmured. 'Not enough sleep.'

His smile was intimate and tender, and she felt her body responding, remembering.

She dragged in a deep, steadying breath. 'I could do with changing,' she said, turning to her mother. 'What if we see you down there at the church in a few minutes?'

'Good idea,' Jake said. 'I'll meet you back here. What do you want to do about the picture?' he added quietly.

'Oh. Can you leave it at yours? I want to give it to them. It can always come back later and go on the dining room wall for Saturday.'

'Sure.' He passed her her bag, winked at her and drove away, and she went inside and found Mel and Tom in the study, Mel sitting on Tom's lap and not very much seating being arranged except their own.

'A-hem,' she said loudly, and they jumped guiltily and giggled like children.

'Nothing is sacred in this house,' Tom complained, and Lydia rolled her eyes.

'There's a time and a place,' she reminded them fondly, and wished she and Jake had the right to such public displays of affection. Not that the study was really public, but—

'How are you getting on?'

'Fine. We're done. Where on earth have you been, you bad girl?' Mel asked, her eyes teasing. 'Mum's been in orbit, and Dad's been grinning and saying about time.'

'Sorry to disappoint you,' she said airily, her heart pounding. 'We got held up because Jake had to go to the office this morning and he couldn't get away.'

'A likely story,' Tom murmured, and patted Mel on the bottom. 'Up you get. I need a drink, I'm parched. Lydia?'

'No, thanks. I've got to change and go up to the church and help with the flowers.'

Mel looked at her and sympathy filled her eyes. 'Are you OK with that?' she asked gently, and Lydia felt a lump form in her throat.

'Yeah, I'm fine,' she said a little gruffly, and turned away. 'I'll go and change. I'll see you in a minute.'

She ran upstairs, tipped her bag out on her bed and pulled on her jeans, then found a fresh T-shirt in a drawer and went back downstairs. Jake was there, dressed in jeans and a polo shirt, looking cool and relaxed and totally at home.

He was drinking a glass of juice, and she took it

from him and finished it without thinking of the intimacy of such a gesture.

'I offered you one,' Tom said in mock indignation, but Mel just looked at her with searching eyes that probably saw too much.

'Come on, they'll be waiting,' she said, and hustled Jake out of the kitchen before Mel could start putting two and two together and coming up with four thousand. It was probably too late, anyway. Oh, damn.

'Look, I know it's probably futile trying to hide anything from my family, but I'd rather they didn't know what happened,' she said as they drove to the church.

'I'd already worked that out,' he replied, and his voice sounded a little taut. 'However, I think your father will see straight through you, and I'm sure Mel knows. Tom is so straightforward if he caught us in bed and we denied it, he'd believe us, but the others are far less naive.'

She disagreed. She thought Tom actually had a great deal more insight than he let on, or else Mel would have been bored with him already. 'Nevertheless,' she went on doggedly. 'I don't want them to know.'

'Relax,' he told her. 'I'm not exactly going to announce it at dinner. ''Oh, by the way, I made love to Lydia all night and then again this morning and again this afternoon.'''

She felt the warmth of desire spreading through her, and closed her eyes. 'I know that,' she murmured. 'It's just—I wanted to keep it private. Between us.'

'And it will be. Don't worry, I won't be swapping stories with Tom.' He sounded edgy, and she felt sorry because she hadn't meant that at all, but there was no point beating it to death. Anyway it was a futile wish, as he'd pointed out, because Mel was much too astute.

It was just that she felt their emotions were so battered and fragile, they needed privacy to explore them, and there was no way anything was private in her family. They were all too darned inquisitive.

They carried all the flowers in from the florist's air-conditioned van, and once that was done they were dispatched to find the parking signs.

'Your father thinks they're in the barn somewhere. If you could find them it would be a help.'

Her heart sank. Yet another reminder—last year's signs.

'Not a problem,' Jake said, propelling her firmly back to the car. She snapped on her seat belt and stared out of the window, unable to hide her feelings, and after a short distance he pulled over.

'Lydia?'

She didn't reply, and he caught her chin with his strong, gentle fingers and turned her to face him. 'They're just bits of wood with paint on, Princess. It doesn't matter. It's in the past. Let it go.'

'It's just—everything is the same,' she said in a choked voice.

'I know. Just ignore it. Put it in perspective.'

She nodded. 'Sorry. You're right, of course.' She tried for a smile, and he winked and leant over to kiss her.

'Attagirl. You'll be all right. It'll soon be over.'

And that, of course, was half the trouble.

They found the signs in the end in the back of the

workshop, stacked behind some sheets of timber, and they cleaned them up and put them in the back of the Mercedes with a mallet and went and hammered them into the ground in the field gateways.

'How many cars are they expecting?' Jake asked, looking at the neatly mown hay field that would be used by the guests.

'Oh, over a hundred. They want the ushers to sort the parking out, I think. At least—'

'That's what they said last year. I know.' His face was tight and closed, and he gave a sign one last hefty whack with the mallet and straightened up. 'Right, that's the lot.'

'All we've got to deal with now is dinner—Aunty Mary's coming, and Aunty Mary isn't known for keeping her opinions to herself. Are you coming?'

He gave a hollow laugh. 'I believe I'm expected. I confess I can hardly wait to meet the old dragon.'

Lydia chuckled. 'Oh, she's not an old dragon. It's the name that does that. She's wonderful. She's just very direct. I usually avoid her like the plague.'

'Direct' was putting it mildly, he thought as the very beautiful and self-possessed widow pinned him against the wall in the kitchen with her piercing green eyes and smiled a gimlet smile.

'So you're Jake,' she said, eyeing him up and down. 'She must have been mad to let you go. I've heard of you—you have a significant reputation.'

He arched a brow, and she chuckled. 'Oh, yes. I know all about you. Your company took over a small firm belonging to my brother-in-law. It was in trouble.

It isn't now, it's turned around and his future is secure, but I gather you take no prisoners.'

He winced inwardly. 'Sometimes you need to be tough to do the job right.'

'Funny, that's what he said. He has great respect for you.'

'Thank you,' he murmured, his smile a little crooked.

'But Lydia, on the other hand, ran away,' she continued thoughtfully. 'Why is that, I wonder?'

'I have no idea,' he said honestly, swallowing the wave of emotion that came up to choke him. It was the absolute truth. Even after the shattering intimacy of last night, he still had no idea.

'Well, ask her,' the invincible Aunty Mary said. 'I take it you have?'

He looked away. 'It was a little difficult. She was on the other side of the world.'

'And it was too much trouble to follow her and talk to her? You're not telling me you couldn't afford the cost—?'

'Aunty Mary, don't be unkind to him,' Mel said, appearing at his elbow like a guardian angel to rescue him. 'He's been very good to me and Tom. I won't let you harangue him.'

'As if I would,' she snorted, and met his eye again. 'Ask her,' she advised, a little more gently. 'The answer might surprise you.'

She walked away, and Mel turned to him. 'What was that all about?'

'Lydia.'

'I might have known. She just can't keep her nose out.'

'She's right,' he said, almost to himself. 'She's absolutely right. Where is Lydia?'

'I don't know. Somewhere—the drawing room, or the conservatory? She was perched on a chair somewhere, trapped by Cousin Alex. You could be kind and rescue her.'

'Aunty Mary's son?' he guessed.

'And her only blind spot. He's the biggest bore in the world. You'd be doing her a favour.'

He found her with a glazed look on her face, a fork suspended halfway to her mouth, and Cousin Alex was in full flood.

'Of course I can't say too much about it, it's all top secret,' he murmured conspiratorially, and Jake rolled his eyes.

'Excuse me interrupting,' he said smoothly. 'Lydia, your mother needs some help.'

'And you are?' Alex asked, head tipped slightly to one side.

'Jake Delaney. Excuse us.'

He left Alex with his jaw still working in shock, and wheeled Lydia through the kitchen and out of the back door.

'What was that all about?' she asked. 'Actually, don't bother, I don't care. I'm just glad you turned up before I stabbed him with my fork.'

'And there I thought you were eating,' he said mildly. 'I've met your Aunty Mary, by the way.'

'Oh, Lord. Sorry.'

'Don't be. She's an interesting woman.'

'Unlike her son,' Lydia said under her breath. 'We're about to get company—my father's brother

Greg and his wife Stella. They're simple, uncomplicated folk. We should be safe.'

Jake didn't want to be safe. He wanted to talk to Lydia, to ask her, as he should have done a year ago, just why she'd walked away.

There was no chance. As they escaped from one conversation they were embroiled in another, and he could tell everyone was fascinated to know just what he was doing there with Lydia.

The family curiosity, he thought, wasn't limited to the immediate members.

Finally he took her by the arm, wheeled her into the downstairs loo and locked the door.

'What the hell are you doing?' she whispered, laughing breathlessly. 'You're crazy. We'll be caught.'

'I'm not doing anything. I just want to talk to you—'

The knob rattled, and someone called 'Sorry!' and went away. Jake sighed. This was neither the time nor the place, but they had to talk, and soon.

'Tomorrow,' he said. 'Can you manage to slip the leash for a while? Come over to my place and we'll talk.'

'We fight when we talk.

'OK. So we'll fight, but we need to talk, Princess. There are things I have to say to you, and I can't do it with your family hounding us and rattling the door-knob—'

Right on cue it happened again, and he rolled his eyes. 'Please. Try and come over.'

'OK.'

The knob rattled again, and someone said, 'Anyone in there?'

'Yes,' they said simultaneously, and then laughed.

'I am never going to live this down,' she said as they escaped past the astonished elderly relative. 'You know what they think we were doing?'

'They're just a few hours too late,' he said softly. 'I'm going home, Princess. Come and see me in the morning.'

'OK.'

'Promise.'

'I promise,' she said with sincerity.

But in the morning she didn't come, because the caterer's van got stuck in the field and everyone had to go and unload all the plates and glasses and cutlery, the table linen, the place mats, the ovens and burners and gas bottles—all had to be brought in a little trailer behind the garden tractor over the bridge, or carried by hand, and it took hours.

And yet again, although they were together, there was no chance to talk at all, and at eleven o'clock he had a phone call from his office to say he simply had to go back, because the general manager and his wife had been killed in an accident.

'I'll be there as soon as I can, Beryl,' he promised his distraught receptionist. 'I'm on my way.'

He found Lydia struggling with a box of table linen, and took it from her.

'That's too heavy for you,' he told her shortly, and dumped it in the kitchen at the back of the marquee. 'Look, I have to go. I've got a crisis at work—my general manager and his wife have been killed and all hell's broken loose.'

'Oh, no, I'm sorry,' she said, her face concerned. 'Are you all right?'

'Yes, I'm fine. A bit shocked—there will be a lot

to sort out, and I have to be there, really. I'm sorry to leave you like this.'

She nodded, and for a fleeting second he thought he saw relief in her eyes, but then it was gone. 'When will you be back?' she asked.

'This evening, I hope. I'll come straight here.'

'We've got the rehearsal.'

Damn. He'd forgotten that penultimate torture. 'I'll be here,' he promised, and, dropping a swift kiss on her lips, he headed off across the lawn at a run.

Lydia watched him go, relief warring with regret. She wanted him there beside her, but as long as he was, she was reminded of the conversation he wanted to have.

If only she knew what it was about, but she was horribly afraid she did know, and didn't like the answer.

'Where's he gone in such a hurry?' Tom asked, pausing beside her with a crate of crockery.

'London. Some crisis at work. His general manager and wife have been killed.'

'Oh, my God. Is he OK?'

Tom's eyes followed him, concerned.

'He said he was. He looked OK. A bit shaken, perhaps.'

'Maybe I should go with him—'

'Tom, you can't leave!' she said flatly. 'Not now! Mum will go into orbit. He said he'll be back for the rehearsal.'

Was there something in her voice? Tom looked down at her and frowned in concern. 'Are you OK?' he asked. 'Really OK?'

She hesitated, swallowing convulsively, and looked

away. 'I'll live,' she said. 'I'll be better when it's over.'

She wasn't sure, as she said it, whether she was talking about the wedding, or her relationship with Jake. She had a horrible feeling she meant both.

It was a sad day in the office. Jake found himself comforting countless employees, all of whom had been very fond of John Trotter and his wife Eileen. They'd been a part of the business almost from the beginning, and he had to bury his personal feelings and help the rest of the company come to terms with their loss.

Beryl, the receptionist, was particularly upset. She'd also been with him since the beginning, and it was John Trotter who'd got her the job. Jake had a great deal of arranging to do to cover John's work-load, as well, dividing it between the few obvious candidates according to their area of expertise and their experience.

It was nearly five before he could get away, and the traffic was hell. It was almost seven by the time he pulled up outside the church, and there would be no time now to talk to Lydia before the wedding.

He wasn't sure he wanted to, now, though. After the shock of John's death, he felt raw and exposed, and the last thing he needed was to hear all about Leo and how much she'd loved him.

Swallowing the pain that thought brought with it, he slammed the car door and headed down the path to the church door.

CHAPTER NINE

LYDIA was exhausted. She'd helped bring all the things across the bridge from the bogged-down caterer's van, which would have been so much easier if they could have used one of the farm tractors, but her father had felt the great chunky tyres would have chewed up the lawn after the rain in the night and he was probably right.

Anyway, everything was across now and the caterers were bustling about and laying the tables in readiness for the following day.

She found herself a chair and sat down, looking around her and trying to keep everything in perspective. It's Melanie's wedding, she kept telling herself. Melanie's wedding. It's going to be all right.

It was certainly going to be spectacular. The marquee was lined, with a tented ceiling and swags along the top of the walls, and the poles were covered in white silky sleeves to disguise the ropes.

It had two doorways with porch-type entrances and real French doors, and one end had been set aside as a reception area where guests could leave their coats and pick up a glass of champagne. The seating arrangements, finalised at last, were up on a board, and the sun was shining through the Georgian-paned PVC windows and making chequered patterns on the rush flooring.

Julie was still arranging the flowers and she looked

dead on her feet, but the arrangements were wonderful, huge hoops around every great pole, bursting with white lilies and sprays of deep green ferns, with accents of red in the flowers and in huge bows set into the midst of the greenery.

Every table had a pot in the centre with matching flowers in it, and the gleaming cloths and sparkling cutlery and glass looked lovely.

'What do you think?' Mel asked, pausing beside her and flopping onto one of the little gold chairs. 'Will it be OK?'

She looked at her sister in amazement. 'Of course it'll be OK. It looks fabulous.'

'Are you sure?'

'Of course I'm sure,' she said firmly, putting her personal feelings aside. 'It'll be wonderful.'

'I hope so. I'm so scared.'

Lydia blinked. 'What? About Tom?'

'No!' Mel laughed at the very suggestion. 'No, about the wedding itself, not about Tom. Never about Tom. Tom's brilliant. He's the best thing that's ever happened to me, and I know you didn't exactly plan it this way, but throwing us together like you did was such a wonderful idea.'

Lydia gave a hollow laugh. 'I'm glad it worked out so well, but I must confess throwing you and Tom together wasn't exactly at the forefront of my mind.'

'I'm sure.' Mel's face was sober and she reached out and covered Lydia's hand. 'Are you all right?' she asked gently. 'About Jake, I mean? I didn't even think when I started planning all this, but it was really very selfish of me, wasn't it, to want to do it the same? It must have made it so hard for you.'

She shook her head in denial, and her fingers threaded through Mel's and clung. 'No. No, darling, it wasn't selfish. It's your big day, Mel, and it's what you want. It was always what you wanted, and you should have it. It isn't the wedding that hurts me, it's losing Jake.'

Mel looked down at their linked hands, covering them with the other one and squeezing. 'I'm sorry. Are you sure you've lost him?'

She nodded. 'He says we have to talk and I know what he wants to say. I spent Wednesday night with him—he just wants to tell me it was goodbye, the close of business. It was something we needed to do, to draw a line under it.'

'But you don't want to,' Mel finished for her.

'No, I don't. I want to live with him for the rest of my life, but it's not going to happen.' She gave a tiny, defeated shrug and tried to pull her hand away, but Mel wouldn't let go.

'Can't you talk to him?'

'And say what? "I know you don't love me, but would you have me anyway?"'

'Are you sure he doesn't love you?'

She shrugged again. 'If he did, surely to goodness he would have said so, and he hasn't, not once.'

'Good grief. Still, I wouldn't be too sure that he doesn't love you. Men are strange. He doesn't talk about himself a lot, not like Tom. Tom's very open about his feelings, but Jake keeps everything to himself. I get the distinct impression that his feelings run very deep, though, like still waters. I think you might find that under all that iron control he really does love you.'

'Then why didn't he say so on Wednesday? There wasn't much evidence of his iron control then, I can assure you!' she said candidly.

'Girls, it's lunchtime,' Maggie called, and Mel stood up.

'Good, I'm starving. Come on, let's go and eat. You'll feel better then; you always do. You're always miserable when you're hungry.'

Lydia went with her, partly because it was the easiest thing to do and partly because she was probably right. There hadn't been a moment for breakfast, and now she was feeling decidedly shaky. She wondered if Jake had got to London, and if he really was all right.

Her father trundled towards them with half a dozen crates of champagne in the trailer on the back of the garden tractor, and paused to speak to them.

'Everything OK?' he asked, and they nodded.

'It's lunchtime. Are you coming in?'

'I'll be up soon. Just get these chilling.'

He drove past them, and they went on up to the house and sat down around the table in the cool, quiet kitchen. Quiet, that was, until everyone arrived and filled it to the gunwales.

'The church flowers look nice,' Maggie said, bustling about with salad and bread and cheese. 'I have to say I think Julie was an excellent choice, Mel, don't you? I just hope the caterers live up to their reputation as well.'

'Let's hope they don't poison us just to get their own back for last year,' Lydia said drily, and they all looked at her in astonishment and then shifted uncomfortably, as if they didn't quite know what to say.

'I think it's unlikely,' Mel said after the silence had stretched on a heartbeat too long. 'Oh, look, Tom, isn't that your parents just arriving?'

Suddenly they were all busy with the new arrivals, and moments later the reunion she'd been dreading was upon her, because Jake's parents arrived, too, and the strained atmosphere was back in force.

'I don't think they'll ever forgive me,' Lydia said *sotto voce* to Mel as they cleared up after the lunch an hour later. 'I'm sure they think it's all my fault and that I'm a flighty little hussy.'

'Probably. I wouldn't give it a second's thought. It isn't them that matter. What does Jake think?'

She shrugged. 'I have no idea.'

'Well, what did he say when you talked about it? You have talked about it, haven't you, since you've been back?'

She shook her head slowly. 'No. Whenever we talk, we fight. We can't seem to find the right words—not to talk about anything that matters, anyway.'

Mel looked thunderstruck. 'I don't believe it. You've slept with him but you haven't even talked about the wedding? Good grief, girl, you must be out of your tree! Why did you sleep with him?'

'Because I didn't want to miss the only chance I thought I'd ever have,' she said frankly. 'That's why, if you want the truth. Because I didn't want to spend the rest of my life wondering what it would have been like.'

'And what was it like?'

She coloured. 'Mel!' she snapped, and scrubbed at a glass with unnecessary vigour.

'Just asking.'

'Well, don't!'

'You shouldn't have told me if you didn't want me to know,' Mel pointed out fairly, and Lydia gave a choked laugh.

'I realise that,' she said, and then dropped the cloth into the water and sighed. 'Oh, Mel, I don't know. I just know I want to spend the rest of my life with him, and it isn't going to happen. He was so irritable after we got back here yesterday, and a couple of times in London, as if I'd really annoyed him. I don't know, maybe it wasn't me, but I think it was.'

Mel shook her head and threw the tea towel onto the front rail of the Aga. 'You two are going to have to learn to talk to each other,' she said bluntly.

'All done, girls?' her mother said, coming back into the kitchen with a groaning tray of coffee cups.

'Oh, no, what's that lot?'

'They can all go in the dishwasher. Don't worry. Thank you for doing that. Are you both OK?'

She hugged them both simultaneously, and Mel slung her arm around Lydia's shoulders to complete the circle.

'Oh, girls, I'm going to miss this,' Maggie said, sounding choked, and Mel hugged them both tight and then stepped away.

'No, you aren't, because I'm going to bring Tom and the children back on a regular basis to annoy you.'

'Children?' Maggie said, her antennae twitching, but Mel flapped a hand at her.

'No, I'm not,' she said laughingly. 'Give us a chance, I'm only twenty-four!'

'But Tom's thirty.'

'I'm sure he'll still be able to manage in a few years, poor old boy,' Mel teased, and Maggie coloured.

'You know what I mean,' she said, giving a flustered laugh, and Mel hugged her again.

'Come on, I've got to go and sit down for a while or I'll be dead on my feet tomorrow.'

'Yes, after all this fuss the bride can't miss the wedding because she's having a lie-in!' Lydia said with a chuckle. 'I'm just going to go upstairs and make sure my dress can hang out properly and hasn't got any creases. I don't want to have to start ironing it tomorrow morning! I'll be down in a bit.'

She ran up the stairs, leaving the chatter and laughter of the guests and her family behind, and closed her bedroom door, leaning back against it with a sigh. She loved them all dearly, but she'd be awfully glad when the wedding was over and everything got back to normal.

Except, of course, it wouldn't be normal because Mel would be in London with Tom. That would feel strange. She'd always been there, except when she was away at university, and they'd been gone at the same time, so it didn't really count.

Still, at least she seemed happy, and Lydia couldn't wish for a nicer man for her than Tom. He was kind, funny, endlessly patient and he obviously adored her.

It was also, equally obviously, mutual.

Lucky pair, she thought again, and turned her attention to her dress. It was hanging in the wardrobe, at the far end. She'd found it last night when she'd put her blue dress away, and she'd meant to get it out this morning to let the creases drop out.

She removed it now, and as she lifted it clear she saw the ghostly gleam of something white behind it.

No, she thought numbly, not white. Off-white, a pale delicate ivory, the colour of frangipani blossom, just touched with oyster.

Slowly, numbly, she took it out and held it up against her, looking at it in the mirror. Made of a lovely heavy pure silk crêpe, it had fine spaghetti straps above a simple neckline that draped softly across the bust. It was cut on the cross to hug her figure, and the hem flared out at the back behind her into a little duster train. She would have worn it with her mother's veil, just a simple fine net that hung softly over her shoulders—the veil that Mel would wear tomorrow.

'But it's so—'

'Simple?' Lydia had said, helping Mel out when she had been, for once, lost for words.

'It's not a wedding dress!'

'Oh, yes it is. I don't want to look like a pavlova!'

'But you could have one of these beautiful ones!'

Like the one hanging on the front of Melanie's wardrobe at that moment, the one she would wear in the morning to marry her beloved Tom. Not a meringue at all, but nevertheless much more elaborate than the one Lydia had chosen.

A lump formed in her throat, and she swallowed it down and shoved the dress back into the wardrobe, her movements jerky. She could deal with it another time. Just now she had to hang the bridesmaid's dress up and hope the creases dropped out by the morning.

By six o'clock, their guests had left for their accommodation and the four of them were sitting down for supper together for the last time. Tom was back at Jake's house with their parents, and it was quiet at last.

'So, young lady, last night at home,' Raymond said, and Mel nodded, her smile tinged with sadness.

'Yes. It seems so strange. I expect I'll be back with Tom every weekend, though, so don't go letting my room!'

They laughed, breaking the melancholic mood, and then predictably talk turned to the wedding and the last-minute organisation. And then, of course, to the rehearsal that was starting in half an hour, and the missing best man.

'Have you heard from him, darling?' Maggie asked Lydia, and she shook her head.

'No. Nothing. He might be home—phone his house. Tom might know where he is.'

'Well, there's no point in worrying. We'll start when he turns up, unless he's going to be very late. We'll ask Tom when he comes over. Raymond, is the marquee all secure?'

'Of course. Everything's locked up, the generator's running, the fridges are on for the champagne and it's all hunky dory. It does look lovely, I must say. You girls have done a wonderful job of planning it.'

There was a tap on the door, and Tom appeared.

'Can I come in?' he asked, smiling diffidently.

'Of course. It's only tomorrow you can't see me,' Mel told him.

'I didn't want to break up the last supper, as it were,' he said with a gentle smile for his bride.

'You're not breaking anything up,' she said, holding out her arms to him, and he hugged her tenderly.

'Any news of Jake?' Maggie asked.

'Yes, he's been stuck in traffic. He said he'd meet us at the church at sevenish. I just thought I'd let you know—that's why I came early.'

'Right,' Maggie said, putting on her organising hat again. 'Let's go down to the church now, then, so we're ready for a prompt start. The vicar said he'd be there from seven. All right?'

It was far from all right, but Lydia knew she'd survive. She'd just have to keep her mind blank and not think too much about it. Then she'd be OK.

His shoes rang on the church floor, echoing in the quietness.

'Ah, the missing link,' the vicar said with a beaming smile and beckoned him in. 'Come in, come in, we haven't started. I was just running through a few things. You know where to stand, I take it?'

He nodded, shooting a quick glance at Lydia and frowning slightly at her pale, drawn face. She looked exhausted—exhausted and emotionally drained, and he should have been here for her.

He took his place beside Tom, and they ran through the service, skipping through the vows and outlining when he would hand over the rings and that sort of thing.

Tom and Mel practised kneeling and standing up without holding onto anything, and then they had to practise leaving the church. He and Lydia had to follow Tom and Mel out, and he offered her his arm. After a heartbeat she rested her slender hand in the crook of his elbow, and he felt a tremor run through her, and frowned again.

'Are you all right?' he murmured, and she shook her head as if to clear it.

'I don't know. I will be once it's all over.'

He didn't want to think that far ahead. He was still reeling from the shock of John and Eileen's deaths, and all he wanted was to lose himself in her arms and howl like a baby.

It wasn't going to happen.

'Jake,' Tom said, released by the vicar at last and coming over to sling an arm around his shoulders. 'Are you OK?'

He nodded, distracted by Lydia slipping away from his side to join her sister. His eyes followed her. 'I'll cope. Are my parents here?'

'Yes, at your house with mine. They're reliving their past. It's nauseating.'

'Right, everyone, can we go back and have just one quick run-through in the marquee, make sure we know where everyone has to be and so on?' Maggie said, and they all obediently trooped back to their cars for the drive to the farm.

His eyes still on her, he saw Lydia getting into her father's car with Mel and closing the door firmly. Tom shrugged and grinned.

'Looks like I've been rejected too. Any chance of a lift?' he asked, and Jake nodded.

'Sure. You can fill me in on what I've missed.'

'Nothing. Your parents and Lydia avoiding each other at lunch, but apart from that, nothing of any moment. Are you really all right?'

The Trotters, he thought with a wave of sadness,

and nodded. 'Yes, I suppose so. A bit shocked. How's Lydia been?'

'Not good. I think she's finding it very hard.'

'She's not alone.'

'This unrequited lust thing can be pretty wearing, can't it?' Tom said with a chuckle, and Jake shot him a startled look.

'I hope you aren't trying to convince me you're talking about you and Mel?' he said drily.

Tom laughed. 'Good Lord, no! No, I was referring to you two, although after Wednesday night I have to say I've got my doubts about the lust being unrequited—maybe it's just the love, but I could have sworn that girl loved you.'

Jake gave a heavy sigh and rammed a hand through his hair. 'I have no idea,' he said flatly. 'I'd like to think so. I hope so, Lord, I hope so, but I don't know. We don't tend to talk about things like that, and Wednesday was no exception. I guess we just take each other's feelings for granted.'

'That might be a bit foolish under the circumstances. Do you have any idea why she went off last year?' Tom asked curiously, and Jake shook his head.

'No, none. We haven't talked about why, just agreed to put it behind us.'

'But you can't, surely to God! Not until you know why. Well, maybe you can, but I couldn't. I'd want to know, chapter and verse, before there was any way I could let her go like that and then risk taking her back.'

'Maybe,' Jake agreed, 'but I have no idea what it was.'

Tom shook his head. 'There must have been something, some pretty compelling reason for her to walk away at that point. She's not an inconsiderate girl, from what I've seen of her and what Mel's said, but she left them with massive bills and hardly any time at all to cancel people's travel arrangements and so forth. You don't do that sort of thing without a very good reason.'

Jake sighed. 'I know. I wish I knew what it was, but there's a bit of me a mile wide that would rather not know and just pretend everything's OK.'

'But it isn't, Jake, and it won't be until you sort it out. You need to talk to her. You never did talk about anything that mattered to you, and it's obvious that she matters, probably more than anything else in your life. Am I right?'

He swallowed hard, and for a second the road swam in front of him. 'Yes, you're right,' he admitted gruffly.

'Of course I am,' his friend said, and put a heavy, comforting hand on his shoulder. 'I think you two are long, long overdue for a heart to heart.'

'But when, Tom?' he said in desperation. 'I know I need to talk to her, I've been trying to do it since yesterday morning, but there just isn't time—well, not the right time, anyway.'

'So make time. Take her to London after we're all finished, and talk to her.'

He shot his friend a jaundiced look. 'My parents are here—I haven't even said hello to them! We should be sitting down together, the six of us, and having a chat and a drink, and comforting you in your hour of need. I can't just disappear!'

'Yeah, you can,' Tom said laconically. 'Our parents are more than happy to talk to each other, and to be honest, Jake, much as I love you, I'd rather spend the rest of the evening with Mel.'

Jake gave a wry laugh. 'Well, that's me told. I'll see. She might not want to talk to me anyway. She seems to be avoiding me, and fate seems to be doing its level best to help her.'

'So hijack her.'

He opened his mouth to protest, then closed it and nodded thoughtfully. 'Nice one, Tom. I might just do that.'

They arrived back at the house, with Lydia suffering waves of *déjà vu*. If only she hadn't panicked last year, maybe it would all have been all right, but she had, and she was no nearer knowing if he loved her now than she had been then.

All she knew now was that she loved him and would love him till she died, but it might not be enough. Sometimes people loved each other but couldn't live together. Sometimes they had wonderful relationships without all the heat and fluster of a love affair.

And sometimes, she thought despairingly, one of them loved more than the other.

The marquee was magnificent. The evening sun streamed through the windows and lit up the table settings and the flowers, and the reception area was all set up ready with trays of glasses, the seating arrangement, coat racks and so forth.

They were all busy admiring it when Tom's and Jake's parents popped their heads round the door.

'May we come in for a sneak preview?' Tom's

mother asked, and they were welcomed with open arms.

'Of course—do come in,' Maggie said, rushing over to them and drawing them inside. 'Jake, your parents are here—I don't suppose you've had time to see them yet?'

'No, I haven't,' he agreed, and she watched as he hugged them affectionately.

'I'm sorry to hear about the Trotters,' his father said, and Lydia saw a flash of pain on Jake's face.

'Yes. It was a—real shock. Um—can we talk about something else?'

He's really hurting, she realised. Poor Jake. I wish I could comfort him.

'Right, let's just sort out this reception line and then we can all go and sit down and have a drink. Mel, Tom, where are you?'

'We're here,' Tom said, emerging from the catering tent with Mel tucked under his arm, looking thoroughly kissed and not the slightest bit abashed.

'OK,' Maggie said, sorting everyone out. 'Raymond, darling, you need to stand here next to me, and Mel and Tom, you need to be there—no, not that way round, the other way round, that's it—and Lydia, you should be here, and Jake, next to her, please—'

Lydia felt the waves of panic rising again. Everyone—absolutely everyone—who was coming to this wedding knew about her and Jake. Most of them had been invited to their wedding last year.

And now she was going to have to stand and smile and talk to them, and all the time she wouldn't know if he cared or not.

She could feel the warmth from his body, smell the

subtle essence of cologne and Jake that made him so distinctive. She ached to throw herself into his arms and beg him to give her another chance, but she couldn't, not in front of all these people.

Maybe not even if they were alone, because she wasn't sure she wanted to know the answer.

She closed her eyes, breathing deeply. Forget yourself, concentrate on doing this. Put it in perspective, she told herself. You can do it for Mel. You can. You can do it—

'I can't do this,' she said under her breath.

'Yes, you can.' Jake's hand found hers, his fingers twining between hers and locking her to his side. 'You can do it.'

'I can't. They're the same people, Jake. What on earth do I say to them?'

'What's the matter, darling?' Maggie asked, looking worried. 'It's so easy. You just have to smile. Nobody will say anything difficult.'

But what will they think? What will I think? That should have been us there, not Mel and Tom, and I threw it all away—

'I'm sorry, I have to get out of here,' she muttered, and pulled her hand free, running for the door.

'Lydia, darling, stop!' her mother called, but she ignored her. Everything was going black, and her ears were roaring, and all she could think about was getting away...

He didn't hesitate. With a grim smile to Tom, Jake strode towards the door, but Maggie intercepted him. 'No! Leave her, you've done enough.'

'No, I haven't,' he said calmly. 'I haven't done

anything like enough. That's the trouble. I'm going to do what I should have done a year ago. She's not running away from me again—not until I know why.'

And very gently but very firmly, he lifted the startled Maggie out of his way and strode out of the door.

'Lydia!' he said, his voice carrying to her as she stumbled across the lawn. 'Lydia, wait!'

'Leave me alone!' she cried, her voice catching.

Damn, she was crying. He might have known that. 'I won't leave you alone, my darling,' he said grimly under his breath. 'Not a chance—not ever again.' He raised his voice. 'Lydia, stop!'

She started to run, heading towards the river across the wild flower meadow, and he followed her, breaking into a sprint and gaining on her rapidly.

She turned, just as he reached her, and her foot caught in the grass and she fell into his arms, knocking him off balance. They tumbled into the wild flowers, his arms still around her, and she pounded her fists on his chest and screamed at him.

'Hush,' he murmured, but she wasn't hushing for anybody.

'Damn you, leave me alone!' she sobbed, but he held her firmly against his chest.

'No, I won't leave you alone. Not until we've talked.'

'We can't talk. We never talk!'

'Yes, we do,' he said in a voice that defied correction. 'And we're going to, just as soon as we're alone. I'm taking you to London.'

She lifted her tear-stained face and stared at him in astonishment. 'London?' she exclaimed. 'We can't go to London! The wedding—'

'We'll be back for the wedding, don't worry, but we're going to have this conversation, and we're going to have it now.'

He got to his feet, scooped her out of the long grass and carried her, kicking and screaming, all the way to his car.

Behind him he could hear Maggie protesting, and someone—Raymond?—laughing.

'Go for it, Jake,' Tom yelled, and someone shushed him, but Jake had no intention of listening to any of them. He had Lydia in his arms, and if he had anything to say about it, that was where she was going to stay for a very, very long time…

CHAPTER TEN

SHE slept in the car. She hadn't thought she would, she was so wrung out with emotion, but he'd refused to talk until they were in London, drowning her protests out with soothing music, and gradually exhaustion and emotion had overcome her. She'd relaxed into the seat, waking only as Jake slid his arms around her and lifted her out of the car.

'Where are we?' she asked, dazed with sleep.

'London.' His voice was grim and brooked no argument, but the fight had gone out of her, and a tiny glimmer of hope was beginning to come to life. If he didn't care, surely he wouldn't go to all this trouble?

He lifted her clear of the car, shut the door with his knee and zapped the remote central locking, then carried her towards the lift like a child.

'I can walk,' she said, her earlier nerves returning, but he just carried on. 'Jake, I've got legs—'

'I have noticed,' he said drily, 'but I've decided I quite like carrying you, so just lie still and relax and enjoy it.'

Enjoy it? Was he mad? Everyone was looking at them, and he just gave them a chilling smile and carried on regardless. Oh, well, at least she had jeans on and they couldn't all see her knickers!

She dropped her flaming face into his shoulder, hung on tight and savoured the masculine scent of him and the feel of his hard, well-muscled body against hers.

Finally she heard the apartment door click softly shut behind them, and he released her legs and set her carefully on her feet.

Was it symbolic, she wondered, or just macho? Or had he been afraid she'd run away again?

He flicked on the lights, flooding the room with a soft, golden glow. 'Can I get you a drink?' he asked, heading for the kitchen.

A drink? How civilised, she thought, a bubble of laughter forming in her throat, but it changed to a tiny sob and she bit her lips.

He stopped in his tracks and turned, staring at her searchingly. 'Lydia?' he murmured. He came back to her, cupping her face with his hands and staring down into her eyes with a racked expression on his face. He sighed softly and wiped a tear from her cheek with his thumb. 'What is it, Princess? Tell me what went wrong.'

But she could only shake her head, too afraid to say the words that would take him away from her.

He tutted gently, and, putting an arm around her shoulders, he led her to the sofa and sat down, drawing her down beside him into the shelter of his side.

'Let me start, then,' he said, his voice low and vibrant with emotion. 'Before we say anything else, and because I want everything that's coming to be in context—I still love you. I didn't stop loving you just because you went away, and I love you now, if anything, even more than I did then.'

Her head flew up and her startled gaze caught his grim, forbidding look—a look she now realised he wore as a mask to hide his feelings. 'Oh, Jake,' she murmured, her heart swelling, but he hushed her.

'I don't know if I've ever told you, but I should have done, and if I've never said it, it's because the words seem so inadequate to describe how I really feel—and anyway, I thought it was obvious, but maybe it wasn't. Maybe I needed to tell you, so I'm doing it now. I'm telling you I love you, that I've loved you since I first met you, and I don't care about Leo—'

'Leo?' she interrupted, yanked off Cloud Nine by this strangely irrelevant connection. 'What's Leo got to do with this?'

'You loved him.'

'No—well, yes, but not like that. Not like I love you. He was just a friend.'

Jake met her eyes, his own burning with some nameless emotion. 'Just a friend? Then—you didn't sleep with him?'

'No. I've never slept with anyone but you.'

His eyes squeezed shut and he dropped his head back and swallowed convulsively. 'Never?' he said in a strangled voice.

'No.' Surely he'd realised? She went on, explaining just in case, 'Wednesday night was the first time I've ever made love to anyone.'

He lifted his head and looked down at her, and the emotion in his eyes was crystal-clear now and made her throat close with love. 'Oh, Princess. I love you so much,' he whispered, and, lowering his mouth, he kissed her tenderly. 'I was so sad. I thought you'd changed your mind when you'd met Leo, and I thought, if only I'd pushed you last year, maybe the lucky man could have been me—and it was me, all along. Oh, sweetheart, I wish I'd known. I would have taken more care with you.'

She gave a sad little laugh. 'More care? I don't think you could have taken more care, but I'm sorry you thought what you did. I imagined you'd realise— I was so naive, so ham-fisted—'

'Ham-fisted?' he exclaimed, and laughed. 'When, exactly?'

She coloured softly. 'Don't be kind. I didn't know what to do—'

He gave a short huff of laughter and hugged her hard against his side. 'You didn't? I'm in real trouble when you've had some practice, then, Princess, because you knocked the feet out from under me, every single time.'

Love filled her heart, and she laughed up at him. 'I did?' she said with a little surge of feminine pride.

'You did. You certainly did.' His smile faded, and he bent his head and kissed her again, his mouth searching for her response. 'Oh, Lydia...'

'Make love to me,' she said, her voice scarcely more than a whisper, and he lifted her into his arms again and carried her up the stairs.

'This is getting to be a habit,' she said with a smile.

'Mmm. I can live with this habit,' he murmured, and lowered her onto the centre of the bed.

'Lydia?'
　'Mmm.'
　'Darling, wake up.'
　'No. Comfy.'
　'Please. We still need to talk.'

This time he got through to her, and she tipped her head back and looked at him in the moonlight. 'OK, I'm awake,' she said softly.

'Last year,' he began, and she could feel the tension in his body. It was hard to miss it, sprawled as she was across him, with her leg flung across his and her arm round his waist and her head on his shoulder. She moved her hand soothingly against his side.

'Go on,' she coaxed.

'Just tell me why,' he said, his voice taut with control.

She sighed. 'Because I didn't think we were doing it for the right reasons—or, at least, I didn't think you were. Well, I didn't know. I mean, your proposal was so throw-away, like a joke, really, and if Mel hadn't come in and heard it and announced it all over the county at the top of her voice, I probably would have realised that—and anyway, I never said yes.'

'I know. You didn't have time, but you seemed to go along with it so happily I thought it was all right, but obviously it wasn't.'

'But it was!' she protested. 'It was all right—for me, anyway. I just wasn't sure you'd meant it, and the more I thought about it, the more worried I became, especially when you didn't tell me that you loved me. Then, at the rehearsal, when we were standing in the marquee on the Thursday, I just felt this terrible panic. I thought, if you didn't love me, if you were just going along with it, then how on earth could I expect our marriage to survive, and I just had to talk to you.'

'And I walked away,' he said slowly. 'Oh, Lydia, why didn't you stop me?'

'I couldn't! You seemed almost relieved that the train had stopped at last, as if you were tied to the track by your own common decency and finally I was giving you an opportunity to get away.'

'That wasn't it,' he told her quietly. 'I had to get away. I didn't know how long I could keep my emotions in check. I hadn't cried since I was nine years old, and I was damned if I was doing it in public.'

'Oh, Jake,' she said sadly. 'I'm sorry. I thought you didn't care. I thought you were relieved and couldn't get away fast enough. I never thought it was that.'

'You wouldn't, would you? Men don't cry.'

'Yes, they do,' she corrected. 'If they care enough about something. But I thought you were just glad it was over. I'd wanted to talk to you, wanted you to tell me not to be silly and of course it would be all right, but you didn't, you just left me there.'

'Because I realised I'd been right. I'd watched you getting more and more tense towards the date of the wedding and I'd managed to convince myself that you were only doing it because you'd said you would, and not because you loved me. I'd hoped I was wrong, that once we were married I'd be able to take you away from all the fuss and woo you back, but then you pulled the plug.'

'I didn't mean to,' she said sorrowfully. 'Oh, darling, I'm so sorry.'

His arms closed around her tighter, and he turned to face her, his eyes extraordinarily intent in the moonlight. 'Lydia, marry me,' he said urgently. 'Please? Marry me and walk beside me through the rest of our lives—have my children, make a home for us all, be there for me to come home to. I need you—

I need you so much, and I swear I'll love you till I die—'

His voice cracked, and her eyes filled with tears.

'Oh, Jake, of course I'll marry you,' she said, and his mouth found hers in a wild and desperate kiss.

'Thank God,' he whispered against her lips, and then he kissed her again, a sweet and tender kiss, trembling with emotion.

She lifted a hand and cradled his jaw, rough with stubble, and looked deep into his eyes. They were still shadowed, and she remembered the tragedy he'd had at work.

'I'm sorry about the Trotters,' she said gently.

His eyes flickered shut, a look of pain crossing his face, and her heart ached to comfort him.

'He was a good man, and his wife was a darling,' Jake said unsteadily. 'They were very kind to me over the years. He gave me my first ever job, when I was fourteen. When I had a chance, I returned the favour, and he never let me down. I just wish I'd told him how much I thought of him—'

A single tear slid from the corner of his eye and left a silver trail in the moonlight.

'Oh, darling, I'm sure he knew,' she murmured, and, sliding her hand up, she cradled his head against her. Then, in the safety of her arms and for only the second time in over twenty years, Jake allowed himself to cry.

'We ought to get up.'

'I know. I promised your mother we'd be back for the wedding.'

'I should be there for Mel.'

'I know.' He turned her into his arms and kissed her lingeringly, then stood up and stretched gloriously.

'I love the view,' Lydia said, admiring him, and he looked through the window.

'It is good, isn't it?'

'I meant you, you fool,' she said, hitting him with a pillow, and he laughed and pulled her up.

'Come on. We've got a wedding to go to—and finally I'm looking forward to it.'

'Me, too,' she said, a big smile spreading across her face. 'Me, too.'

They threw on their clothes, had a glass of orange juice from the fridge and left, just as the first rays of sun streaked across the room and turned it gold. By the time they got back to Suffolk Maggie was panicking, and her face when she saw them was comical.

'Hello, darling,' she said cautiously, eyeing them both a little uneasily.

'Hello, Mum. Be nice to Jake,' she warned. 'He's going to be your son-in-law.'

'Thank God for that,' Raymond said, coming in behind them and clapping Jake on the back. 'About time, son. Welcome back to the family.'

'Thank you,' he said softly, and smiled down at Lydia. 'Darling, I have to go. Tom will be flapping. I'll have to go and dress him and calm him down, and his mother won't be helping because she'll be in tears about her little boy, if I know her. I'll see you in the church.'

'OK.' She drew his face down for a kiss, and when she let him go she saw Mel standing in the doorway, her eyes filled with tears.

'Is it all right?' she asked, and when Lydia nodded, she burst into tears.

'Oh, I'm so glad,' she cried, and Lydia hugged her and cried too, and then Maggie joined in, and Raymond cleared his throat and reminded them all that they had a wedding to go to.

'Oh, good grief, we're going to be late!' Mel shrieked, and Lydia ran upstairs after her and calmed her down. She showered at the speed of light, dragged a comb through her damp hair and changed into her clean underwear, then went into Mel's room in her dressing gown.

'OK, sis, I'm all yours. What do you want me to do?'

'Tell me all about last night,' Mel said drily, smoothing on her foundation. 'But I don't suppose you will.'

'No, I won't.'

'But I take it he does love you.'

'Oh, yes,' Lydia said softly. 'He loves me. We're getting married—I don't know when.'

'You ought to get married today,' Mel said, peering at her eye and smudging soft colour onto the lid.

'It's your day,' Lydia said firmly. 'When it's all over, then we'll get married.'

'Well, don't you dare do it while we're away—you know we're going for three weeks, don't you?'

'Yes, I know.'

'I'll kill you if I miss your wedding,' Mel threatened.

'You won't miss it—but you might miss your own if you don't get a wiggle on.'

*   *   *

It was a beautiful wedding. Lydia sat on one side of the aisle, with Jake on the other, and if their attention was more on each other than on the bride and groom, nobody really noticed.

Lydia had her hands folded in her lap and her fingers played with her engagement ring, back where it belonged. Jake had been waiting for her arrival at the church, had come out into the sunshine, led her round the corner out of sight and slipped it on her finger with a gruff, 'That's better.'

There was still a faint trace of lipstick on his cheek, Lydia noticed with a smile, but she didn't care and she didn't suppose he did either. She looked down at the ring, perfect in its simplicity, a beautiful diamond in a very plain setting, with nothing to detract from its natural beauty.

And soon it would be joined by the wedding ring, sitting in his drawer at home, he'd told her, snuggled up on its satin bed next to the one he would wear.

She couldn't wait. She was longing for the moment she would be his wife, and they could settle down in his lovely house and plan their future.

First on the list, she decided, was one of Molly's niece's puppies, a sister to the one her mother would have, followed by lots of lovely little children, chubby babies with Jake's amazing eyes and masses of soft, dark hair.

Beautiful children. They couldn't fail if they took after their father, she thought proudly, and caught his eye. He winked, and she smiled, unaware of the interested looks they were attracting, and after only a few more minutes they were walking down the aisle, her hand tucked in the crook of his arm, and she thought if he looked any more handsome her heart would burst with pride.

She was stunning. Jake stood beside her in the receiving line with his arm firmly round her, smiling at all the guests and defying them to comment. They didn't—not directly—but plenty was said as the guests walked away.

Her mother was blotted up and smiling again after her tears of pride in the church, and her father was looking distinctly nervous as his time drew nearer.

Jake hadn't even thought about a speech, but it didn't matter. Public speaking was something he'd always been good at, and he'd meant to put a few ideas down last night, but he'd been otherwise engaged in the end.

Ah, well. He had a few ideas, and he could make a note or two during the course of the meal.

He was next to Lydia, of course, in accordance with tradition, and he sat with his leg firmly up against hers and jotted down ideas. Her father started the ball rolling with some touching remarks and gentle teasing, and Mel laughed and her eyes filled at his loving words.

Then Tom rose and did the 'My wife and I' joke, and then it was Jake's turn.

He was very conscious of everyone's curiosity, and he started with a joke at his own expense.

'I'm sure you were all very relieved when you arrived and found there was still a wedding to attend,' he said, and there was a ripple of nervous laughter. He smiled encouragingly. 'That's because despite our traditional titles my friend is very definitely the best

man, a much better man than I and infinitely more
capable in matters of the heart. He's also much more
organised than I am, and, just in case, he had the
foresight to confiscate his intended's passport.'

That brought a deep chuckle, and he relaxed and
threw himself into the customary tale-telling, dredging up stories from their very early past, and others,
stories of more recent origin, that brought the house
down.

Winding up, he said, 'We've lived together off and
on for a long time. He's been a good friend, and between me and his mother I think we've got him pretty
well house-trained. I have to say I think Melanie has
chosen well, and if he knows what's good for him,
I'm sure he won't give his lovely bride a moment's
worry.'

There was another ripple of laughter, and he drew
a deep breath. 'Now, tradition has it that I should at
this point draw your attention to the bridesmaid, and
ask you to agree with me that she's looking beautiful
today. Isn't she lovely, ladies and gentlemen?'

There was a murmur of approval that brought soft
colour to Lydia's cheeks, and he looked deep into her
eyes, and went on, 'I think so, anyway, but then I'm
biased. I happen to love her.' There was a gasp, and
he looked back over his audience and lifted his champagne. 'Ladies and gentlemen, please raise your
glasses and drink a toast with me—to Lydia.'

'To Lydia,' they echoed, and the applause was
deafening.

Her cheeks were pink, and her eyes sparkled with
tears. 'You rat,' she scolded laughingly as he
sat down.

'It's true. You couldn't have me stand in front of all these people and lie, could you?' His heart faltered. 'Or didn't you mean it when you said you love me?' he said, suddenly serious.

'Of course I meant it. Don't doubt me, Jake. I'll love you for ever.'

'That's a long time.'

'I know.'

He felt the tension drain away, and he smiled. 'I love you, Princess,' he murmured.

'I am going to get you,' Tom said, leaning over towards him and laughingly levelling a finger at him. 'Fancy bringing up the teddy bear!'

'I can think of far worse things,' he chuckled, leaning back and relaxing again. 'Count yourself lucky.'

'Come on, you two, you need to go and circulate,' Maggie prompted, and then the party became much less formal. Everyone was having a wonderful time, and even Lydia seemed to be enjoying it, up to a point, but Jake could tell when she'd had enough and he took her firmly by the hand and led her outside into the garden.

'Let's go under the willow,' she suggested, and they strolled over there hand in hand, past the spot where they'd fallen in the wild flowers the previous evening. Once under the shelter of the tree, she turned to him and looked up at him with love in her eyes, and he felt his heart lurch.

'Kiss me,' she ordered.

'My pleasure.' He drew her into his arms for a long, leisurely kiss, not a prelude to passion but a gentle sharing.

'I love you,' he murmured, brushing her hair back from her face and kissing her again.

'I love you, too. I wish we'd said that last year. All the time we've wasted.'

He shook his head, dismissing it. Life was too short for regrets. 'We're together now; that's all that matters. Just me and you.'

'I wish we could get married just like that,' she said wistfully, clicking her fingers, 'instead of all this fuss.'

He sighed. He'd always known she didn't want all the hullabaloo, but he realised he had no idea what she would have chosen in its place. 'What would you really like?' he asked carefully. 'If you could choose anything, what would it be?'

'Really? I'd like to get married here, under this tree, right now. In fact,' she said, looking around her, 'we could do it. Mel said she'd kill me if we got married before they got back, but they're here now, and so are your parents and mine, and the vicar. Why don't we just do it—have a simple ceremony, here, now, just with them?'

He felt his jaw sag a fraction. 'You are one crazy woman,' he told her, a slow smile spreading over his face and a strange excitement building in his gut. 'Anyway, it won't be legal without the banns or a registrar—'

She flapped a hand at him, brushing that weak argument aside. 'That doesn't matter. I'm not worried about the law. It's our vows that matter, Jake,' she said earnestly. 'I love you, and I want you to know that. '

For an age he hesitated, then he laughed softly.

'OK. I'll talk to Tom, see what he thinks. We might be able to sneak out without the others seeing us.'

'When they go to change—nobody will be expecting any of us around then, and we could get away with it, if we could creep back down here somehow. There's a path at the other end of the garden. We could come down that way and meet the vicar and our parents under the tree.'

He nodded. 'I've got the rings in the house; I can soon get them. What about your wedding dress?'

Her eyes filled. 'I've still got it,' she said. 'It won't fit so well, I'm thinner.'

'I'm sure it will be fine.' He could feel excitement building, and he hugged her. 'Let's go and talk to Tom and Mel.'

'I don't want to steal their thunder,' Lydia said worriedly. 'We mustn't say anything to anyone else.'

'I agree. It's their day, but it could be ours too. Let's go and find them and see what they think—and it might be an idea to check with the vicar!'

'Of course it fits! It's cut on the cross; it can't fail. Oh, Lydia, you look lovely.'

Mel pinned the veil, so recently on her own head, onto Lydia's, and tucked some of the wild flowers she'd brought up with her into the crown. 'There,' she said with satisfaction. 'Twice in one day—that must be a record for a family veil!'

Lydia laughed breathlessly. 'I can't believe we're doing it,' she said.

'Girls?' Tom called. 'Are you ready?'

'Yes—send Jake down to the marquee to get the

parents and the vicar,' Mel called. 'We'll go the other way and see him down at the tree.'

Mel pulled her jacket on, checked her appearance quickly in the mirror and grinned. 'I think this is excellent. Well done,' she said with a laugh, and Lydia was hugely relieved to see her happiness.

'Are you sure we aren't treading on your toes?' she asked once more, and Mel rolled her eyes.

'Absolutely not!' she protested. 'Come on, you can't get out of it like that.'

'I don't want to,' Lydia assured her fervently.

They hurried down the side of the garden, Tom going ahead as a lookout, and then they were there, and she was on her father's arm miraculously, and Melanie was standing behind her.

As she drew level with Jake, he handed her a posy of wild flowers, tied with a ribbon stolen from a flower arrangement, and his smile warmed her to the bottom of her heart.

'Are you sure?' he said softly, and she nodded.

'Oh, yes. I'm sure.'

So, for the second time that day, the few people gathered there heard the wedding vows repeated, and when they were concluded, the vicar smiled at them and said with great feeling, 'Congratulations. I hope you'll be very happy together; you deserve it. God bless you both. Jake, I think you'd better kiss your bride.'

He looked down at her, his eyes full of tenderness, and, bending his head, he kissed her with all the love in his heart.

Then she was hugging and kissing her mother and her sister and receiving congratulations and kisses from Jake's proud parents. Lydia's father was beaming and looking totally bemused, and then Tom glanced at his watch.

'I hate to nag, but we're going to miss our flight if we don't head off. We'd better go back in.'

People were looking at them as they went back to the marquee, puzzling over Lydia's change of dress, and then Tom stood on a chair and bellowed.

There was instant silence, and he grinned at the astonished company. 'Ladies and gentlemen, I hope you've all still got something in your glasses,' he announced, 'because while you've all been having fun in here, there's been another wedding. Could I ask you, please, to raise your glasses and make a toast, ladies and gentlemen? To Lydia and Jake.'

'Lydia and Jake?' they all cried, and there was a huge surge of noise as they all clamoured to know just what had happened.

'Fancy a lift?' Tom said with a grin, and they set of at a run, though a tunnel of guests armed with confetti, up the lawn and into the waiting bridal car.

'Can we squeeze in another pair?' Tom asked, and the driver grinned and nodded.

'Bouquet!' Maggie called, and Mel turned back and arched her bouquet over the heads of the crowd.

'Right. Let's go!' Tom said, and the driver pulled away. Cameras were clicking, but the two couples inside were oblivious.

'Fancy a lift to London?'

'My house will do,' Jake murmured, holding Lydia firmly at his side. 'I need to fax the estate agent and tell him there's been a change of plan...'

Celebrate the season with

Midnight Clear

A holiday anthology featuring
a classic Christmas story from
New York Times bestselling author

Debbie Macomber

Plus a brand-new *Morgan's Mercenaries* story
from *USA Today* bestselling author

Lindsay McKenna

And a brand-new *Twins on the Doorstep* story
from national bestselling author

Stella Bagwell

Available at your favorite retail outlets in November 2001!

Where love comes alive™

Visit Silhouette at www.eHarlequin.com

PSMC

Marriages meant to last!

They've already said "I do," but what happens
when their promise to love, honor and cherish
is put to the test?

Emotions run high as husbands and wives
discover how precious—and fragile—
their wedding vows are....
Will true love keep them together—forever?

Look out in Harlequin Romance® for:

HUSBAND FOR A YEAR
Rebecca Winters (August, #3665)

THE MARRIAGE TEST
Barbara McMahon (September, #3669)

HIS TROPHY WIFE
Leigh Michaels (October, #3672)

THE WEDDING DEAL
Janelle Denison (November, #3678)

PART-TIME MARRIAGE
Jessica Steele (December, #3680)

Available wherever Harlequin books are sold.

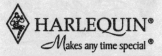

*Together for the first time
in one Collector's Edition!*

New York Times bestselling authors

Barbara Delinsky

Catherine Coulter Linda Howard

Forever Yours

**A special trade-size volume containing three
complete novels that showcase the passion,
imagination and stunning power that these
talented authors are famous for.**

Coming to your favorite retail outlet in December 2001.

HARLEQUIN®
Makes any time special ®

Visit us at www.eHarlequin.com

PHFY

Harlequin Romance ®

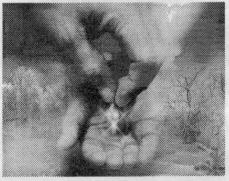

THE AUSTRALIANS

MEN WHO TURN YOUR WHOLE WORLD UPSIDE DOWN!

Look out for novels about the Wonder from Down Under—where spirited women win the hearts of Australia's most eligible men.

Harlequin Romance®:

OUTBACK WITH THE BOSS
Barbara Hannay (September, #3670)

MASTER OF MARAMBA
Margaret Way (October, #3671)

OUTBACK FIRE
Margaret Way (December, #3678)

Harlequin Presents®:

A QUESTION OF MARRIAGE
Lindsay Armstrong (October, #2208)

FUGITIVE BRIDE
Miranda Lee (November, #2212)

Available wherever Harlequin books are sold.

HARLEQUIN®
Makes any time special®